The Auschwitz Violin

Maria Àngels Anglada

Translated by Martha Tennent

corsair

Constable & Robinson Ltd
3 The Lanchesters
162 Fulham Palace Road
London W6 9ER
www.constablerobinson.com

Originally published as *El violi' d'Auschwitz*
by Columna (in Catalan), 1994

First published in translation in the US by Bantam Books,
an imprint of The Random House Publishing Group,
a division of Random House, Inc., New York, 2010

First published in the UK by Corsair,
an imprint of Constable & Robinson Ltd, 2010

This paperback edition published by Corsair, 2011

A copy of the British Library Cataloguing in
Publication Data is available from the British Library

A-format edition ISBN: 978-1-84901-982-8
B-format edition ISBN: 9-781-84901-981-1

Typeset by TW Typesetting, Plymouth, Devon

Printed and bound in the UK

1 3 5 7 9 10 8 6 4 2

To the victims

In memoriam

The Auschwitz Violin

I

Guard Duty, Ghetto 6
Litzmannstadt, December 1, 1941

Incident: use of firearm

On December 1, 1941, I was on duty at guard post 4 on Hohensteinerstrasse from 1400 hrs. until 1600 hrs. Around 1500 hrs. I noticed a Jewish woman walking along the ghetto border. She stuck her head out between the bars and was trying to steal turnips from a parked cart. I fired my rifle. The Jewish woman was mortally wounded.

Type of firearm: carbine 98
Ammunition used: two cartridges

Signed:
Naumann
Reserve Guard
1st Company, Ghetto Bn.

December 1991

I always have trouble falling asleep after I perform at a concert. It keeps playing in my mind, like a tape going round and round. I was more keyed up than usual because this concert had been special: it marked the two hundredth anniversary of Mozart's death. The recital was held in Krakow, a city of wonderful musicians, in a makeshift auditorium in the *bellísima* Casa Veneciana. The extreme cold had kept us from visiting much of the art-strewn city; but at noon, when the fog lifted and the sun appeared, I was able to slip out of the hotel for a stroll along Ryneck Glowny.

The concert was dedicated to Mozart, but the pianist in our trio, Virgili Stancu, had reluctantly accepted the Polish organizers' suggestion to include Chopin's preludes for the first part of our program. This he did with his usual virtuosity, his fingers well acquainted with the pieces. For the second part, he and I played the *Sonata in B-flat*, which Mozart had written for Regina Strinasacchi, the violinist he had so admired. We stayed after completing our part in order to hear the orchestra's impeccable interpretation of the *Sinfonia Concertante, K. 364*. It was a wonderful piece that highlighted the rich flats while subtly suggesting the dramatic nature behind the wise, graciously intertwined phrases.

My attention was particularly drawn to the beautiful tone quality of the solo violin played by a mature woman, the orchestra's first violinist. Her performance was extremely accomplished, and she displayed tremendous, barely restrained passion. I couldn't help noticing that her eyes grew sad when she stopped playing.

It was late at night, and I couldn't sleep. I could still hear the sound of the violin. Not that it was powerful, but it *was* velvety and full. Of course, it was not one of the instruments made by the great masters of Cremona. It occurred to me, though, that it might have been a violin from the old Polish school. Could a Mateusz Dobrucki of Krakow have survived so much ruin? As I pondered the mystery of the woman's violin, it struck me that hers was a darker red, not as transparent as a Dobrucki. It was not implausible that it was German, or Tyrolese, made by one of the Klotzes, the long line of violin makers.

'No, no, Climent. As you can see, it's not a Klotz.'

Regina said it with a smile, but no joy lay behind the smile. It was the day after the concert. To keep my mind off the performance, I'd buried myself the night before in an excellent thriller by Eric Ambler, always a guarantee of deep, peaceful sleep, but I had decided that I would ask the violinist about the origins of her instrument.

We met at the city's Academy of Music (they don't call it a conservatory), where I had been invited to teach a class. I admired the oil portraits in the spacious vestibule: the whole series of magnificent Polish musicians, from the oldest down to my colleague Wienasky. Then I was led to a smallish room to deliver a 'magisterial lesson,' a master class as they call it today.

When the lesson finished, Regina placed her violin in my hands. I tried it, and the strings responded to my every appeal, like pliant clay being molded in my hands. It was marvelous.

'I don't suppose you'd be willing to part with it?'

'Not for anything in the world,' she replied. 'Not even if I were starving to death. It's all that remains of my family. My uncle Daniel made this violin, made it to the same measurements as the Stradivarius. I wouldn't exchange it for any other!'

'Of course not. I can understand how you treasure it.'

'No, no, you can't understand. You'd have to know the whole story.'

A shadow of sadness swept across her blue eyes, accentuating the wrinkles on her beautiful face. She ran her hand through the tufts of her blond, dawn-streaked hair. Her breathing was fast and heavy.

We were unable to continue our conversation because I had promised to attend a performance given by the older string music students in the Main Hall. Regina came with me. The students played the *Intermezzo* by Penderecki, who had been rector of the Academy of Music for many years. The performance was followed by a reception, but Regina seemed to find it tiresome.

'Have you had enough of the party?' she asked.

The reception had hardly begun and I wasn't at all tired, but she had stirred my curiosity.

'It suits me fine to leave; I've finished what I came to do. I'll take you home, if you like.'

She lived near the Academy of Music, and we decided to brave the cold afternoon and walk through the fog, which had again settled on the city. She invited me up for tea. It was a small, simple apartment: life was hard in Poland. I didn't mention her violin again; I wanted to distract her, talk about other things. She spoke of her son, showed me his picture and explained that he was living in Israel. But she didn't want to leave Krakow to join him.

'What would I do there?' she said. 'He's a diamond cutter and has a good job, but Israel has so many musicians now, especially Russians. They could form a hundred orchestras! He'll be coming for the New Year, for Rosh Hashanah.'

Right away we began to talk music. We discussed certain interpretation problems while we listened to a recording of the Sinfonia Concertante. She proved to be a superior pianist as well, and we ended up playing together – this always happens to me. The piano occupied half of her dining-living-music room; it was all one area. Playing together brought us closer than hours of conversation ever could have, and I realized we were becoming friends. For a brief moment her cheeks were ablaze, and I thought I could read, like a passing breeze, a spark of desire in her eyes. Was I being presumptuous? Was it just the music? My God, I thought, she's much older than me!

By the time we had finished the sonata, she was transformed, full of laughter. She closed the piano and was holding my hands with delight when the phone rang. She was in even better spirits when she hung up. She didn't have to offer an explanation, but she disclosed that it was her friend. 'He's not a musician,' she added. 'He's an industrial technician, works at Nowa Huta. We aren't able to go out much together.'

It was getting dark, and I had to make my way back to the hotel where Gerda, our cellist, and Virgili were waiting for me. Regina and I parted reluctantly and agreed that the four of us would have dinner the following night at the hotel where Gerda, Virgili and I were staying. I didn't want Regina to have to spend any money; she was an excellent professional musician, but I knew that earning a living through music wasn't easy. It occurred to me that we could invite her to Holland for a joint concert. I didn't want to mention it without consulting the others in the trio, but I felt sure they would agree. They too had praised her performance.

I offered to take her home after our dinner the following night, but she said it wasn't necessary; it'd be too late for me. She did, however, allow me to call her a taxi and let me pay for what I knew would be more than the fare back. We said goodbye with a warm, friendly embrace, and I thought for a moment with regret about her soft body and how desirable it must have been some years before.

She had spent almost the entire meal talking to Gerda rather than to me. They'd even wandered off together for a long while. When they returned I realized that Regina had changed into one of Gerda's concert dresses, a dark blue one with stripes that flattered her. I assumed they had shared other secrets as well, and the next day I learned that I wasn't mistaken.

'Regina was so pleased with your comments on the interpretation!' Gerda exclaimed. 'And by the class you gave the older students. She was extremely impressed.'

'Well, to be honest, I'm not sure how helpful it was. You heard how they played.'

'But, Climent, you provided them with a new point of view; your approach is quite different from that of the academy here. She found it really stimulating, especially the part about cadence.'

Gerda paused and changed the subject. 'Did she tell you anything about her life?'

'No, and I didn't ask. I'd never be that indiscreet! Besides, I think it would have disturbed her. When she mentioned that her uncle Daniel had made her violin, she murmured in a low voice: "May his memory be for a blessing."'

'You're right,' Gerda confirmed. 'She would have been distressed: practically her entire family were victims of the Holocaust. Her mother and grandmother died in the Krakow ghetto, her father and older brother at Auschwitz, all of them killed by the Nazis.'

How young she must have been at the time. How did she manage to survive? I could only suppose that Regina's love of music had helped to stanch the pain of all those somber shadows.

'She left these photocopies for you, material she collected from those years. She said you'd shown interest in her violin, and the papers would help you re-create part of its story.'

I glanced at the papers, pleased that she had sent them, a sign of true friendship.

'Did you read it?'

'It kept me up most of the night. But she asked me to give it to you; it's all yours now.'

We had convinced Regina to join us in a series of concerts, once we managed to work out the details. Gerda had discussed it with her, and she always gets her way. We had agreed to perform Beethoven's *Archduke Trio* in one of the concerts, and Regina would play the violin part. I was happy for her to take my place. Our agent, Gerda's brother, would arrange the rest of the details. Regina had rarely left the country, and some days abroad would be good for her. She would come for three weeks, she had told us, but no longer: 'People are too envious of my teaching post.'

Our concert tour was drawing to a close; one last recital in Warsaw and then we would separate: Gerda and Virgili would be heading to Amsterdam and I back to my studio in Paris, where I was scheduled to record a CD.

We were stuck at the Warsaw airport for more

than two hours because of the fog, and I passed the time studying Regina's notes, her rough English translation. I perused a few pages and thought to myself, I'll send the papers on to Maria Àngels, she'll find this interesting, but then I forgot everything as I concentrated on the notes. One name appeared often, and it wasn't unfamiliar. My colleagues had to warn me that my flight had been announced; I hadn't even heard it, absorbed as I was in the story of my friend's violin. A story I will never forget.

II

And to a place I come where nothing shines.

– DANTE, *Divine Comedy, Inferno*, canto 4
  translated by Henry Wadsworth Longfellow

Procedures for Punishment and Lashes – 1942

ARREST
*First class (normal): Up to 3 days. Windowed cell.
Wooden bunk. Rations: bread and water. Full meal
every four days.
Second class (aggravating circumstances): Up to 42
days. Dark cell. Wooden bunk. Rations: same as for first
class.
Third class (rigorous): Up to 3 days. No sitting or lying
down. Dark cell. Rations: same as above.*

CORPORAL PUNISHMENT
Number of lashes: 5, 10, 15, 20, 25
Instructions: Medical checkup required before administering punishment.
A leather whip will be used to apply lashes without pauses; each lash will be counted. It is forbidden to strip or uncover any part of the body. The person is not to be tied up but will lie across a bench. Lashes will be applied to hips and buttocks only.

Stamp
THE SS ECONOMICS AND ADMINISTRATIVE DEPARTMENT
(WVHA)
. . .

Calculation of SS earnings based on the employment of camp prisoners
Average salary: 6 Reichsmarks
Deduction for food: 0, 60 RM
Deduction for amortization of clothes: 0, 10 RM
Average life of prisoner: 9 months = 270 days
$270 \times 5.30 \text{ RM} = 1.431 \text{ RM}$

When Daniel emerged from the cell where he had been imprisoned – or, more accurately, when he was dragged from it – he felt much weaker, although only four days had elapsed. He was tempted to curse the determination that had kept him alive and in this hell. He knew it had been four days; he had kept count: each evening he had made a small incision in the wall with his fingernail.

Guards never offered explanations and rarely followed regulations. Daniel and his bunkmate had overslept that bleak, wintry morning and were not out of the dilapidated barracks on time: this was their crime and their misfortune. His body still ached from the whipping he had received before he was locked up, and from sleeping on a hard, short bunk. He figured that the bunk had been built too short on purpose.

Daniel was more fortunate than most prisoners. He enjoyed a privileged position, if you could call it that: he was on his way to the Commander's house, where he had been assigned to work. Were it not for that, who knows how long his punishment might have lasted? As he walked, he blew on his fingers, which had grown numb from the cold. Months had passed since he had last recited the *Shaharit*, the ancient morning prayers he had learned as a child. Standing outside for roll call had made him even colder, but as he started work he was reminded that at least he would have a warm meal again: watery turnip soup.

The punishment cells were located near Appell-platz, the square where public executions were staged. It was the highest elevation in hell. The Dreiflüsselager – the Three Rivers Camp, one of the relatively small Auschwitz subcamps – seemed huge as it stretched out below him, almost imperceptible under a mantle of fog; its ominous buildings were shrouded in shadows. The roofs of the barracks were chalky white, from snow or frost, he wasn't sure which.

Commander Sauckel, a refined but sadistic giant of a man, was determined to cultivate gladioli and camellias, and Daniel and his fellow workers had labored for some time over the wooden structure of the greenhouse. Occasionally this work procured them an extra ration of food. Fortunately, Daniel thought to himself, they hadn't offered him one last 'souvenir' of his arrest: the beating fre-quently dispensed when you were released. You could never be sure of anything here; these camps were separated from the others, and regulations were often ignored.

He'd learned that lesson just four days before, when he'd been forced to watch other prisoners be whipped before it was his own turn to be 'punished.' Daniel laid himself across the bench before they had a chance to pin him down. He pulled his shirt up and trousers down. Gripping the bench, he cried out one thing alone: the number of each of the twenty-five lashes. His body ached with intolerable pain, but he never lost count, so the flogging did not recommence, as was often the case – much to the guards' amusement. He had been able to escape the 'formal' whippings until then, but there was no way to avoid being thrashed and shoved by the guards. With only a cursory glance, the camp's cold, steel-eyed doctor had stamped his approval: Daniel and his fellow inmate would receive corporal punishment. As far as anyone could recall, approval was given to all punishments. Then the doctor had scrutinized him carefully, and the expression on his face had sent shivers through Daniel. Who knew if he was being considered for some future experiment?

The veteran inmates spoke of a worse hell, one-way journeys that took place in other camps, terror-inspiring names and also a beggarly paradise:

the factory where extra rations were served and no one was mistreated. Daniel, however, wished to be neither more frightened than he already was nor swept away by dreams: his job had to be done carefully, and he was finding it especially hard today. He had been given even less bread in the confinement cell than the usual ration, barely enough to keep him alive. He applied himself to the job as best he could, rarely stopping to rest, pleased, in any event, that he had not been sent to the quarry. As he worked he recalled the sudden impulse that had saved his life. Though for how long he didn't know.

'Occupation?'

The question had seemed inoffensive enough, but not everyone had the good fortune to be asked. Those who were selected immediately to die – children, old men and women, the infirm – stood in another line.

Daniel was quick to reply:

'Carpenter, cabinetmaker.'

It was a half-lie. The answer had risen from deep within the recesses of his mind; only later would he reason it out. It was as if someone had dictated it to him. In those days, when persecution had grown more inexorable than ever, you had to walk a tightrope in order to live, but Jews were marked and were – like many others – poor funambulists. He was well acquainted with those who spun the destiny of his people: the murderous Waffen-SS officers, monsters disguised as men, impeccably dressed – unless bespattered by blood – well groomed, often quite cultured men who probably loved their dogs and music, family men no doubt. From their serene (or fanatical) eyes and delicate, heinous hands hung a thin thread: life or the illusion of it. For these Christians, these *goyim* – he thought in a flash, as he heard the question – the ancient commandment 'Thou shalt not kill' did not exist. The question was never posed to his mother. Reduced to a mere husk of her former self, she had died in the ghetto early on. Her Jewish doctor could do nothing; the word *tuberculosis* was mentioned, but Daniel always assumed that his mother had died of hunger or grief.

What could a luthier, a violin maker, do in hell? 'Carpenter' had seemed like a good answer at the time, even to the official who registered the information with an approving nod. Always a need for one. But after a few harrowing months, which had seemed more like years, Daniel was no longer certain. At least his *occupation* meant he was released from the 'windowed cell' after only a brief stay, and now he was out in broad daylight. The cell had only one tiny window, so the days had been spent in semidarkness. The officials spoke of regulations, but no one ever knew how long confinement would last.

Daniel was conscious of the advantage he had over most prisoners: he worked inside, now that the greenhouse was almost completed. He was putting the finishing touches on a bottle shelf in the cellar. He had heard snatches of conversation about more odd jobs around the house; maybe he would be fortunate enough to be assigned to one.

If I'm falling asleep, he thought, it must be because I'm not eating enough and I'm compensating for the lack of food with sleep. It was still dark when the prisoners rose at half past five, ready to begin work at six forty-five. Others had only a half-hour rest at noon, but those who worked in the Commander's house or office had an hour, provided the job had been done according to the officer's demanding, erratic liking. The afternoon shift continued until half past six, stopping in time for the meager supper, then the extremely long roll call and night, with never the hope of a more benevolent dawn. On Sundays, however, those working at the Commander's house began their day later. Having spent his Saturday nights either out late or engaged in his little orgies at home, Sauckel wanted no early-morning noise, no disturbances. These small advantages – cloaked always in the fear that they could end in an instant – were the only positive thoughts Daniel conceded. Never allowing himself to think beyond the moment, ignoring even the shooting pain that occasionally ravaged his body. Never allowing himself to miss Eva, who was perhaps dead, or recall that they would be married now if it hadn't been for the war. Not remembering their introduction according to the community customs, or her last embraces, or how warm her lips had grown after the first weeks of their formal relationship.

His weakness was so acute today that the idea of feeling desire struck him as something from another life, another person. Only his rage kept him from collapsing; he didn't want to become a spectacle for the Führers, the kapos, the vicious horde of hyenas. Against his will, he found himself thinking of the first weeks of confinement in Dreiflüsselager and the secret encounters with female prisoners – the furtive, rapid contacts at night behind the compound wall. Soon, however, men and women were separated by an electric fence that the prisoners had installed themselves. Daniel was young and lively by nature, but he had so little stamina that it had hardly mattered to him.

He was hungry again. The noon meal could only momentarily salve one's hunger, never resolve it. Perhaps the cook would save him some crumbs today; she had risked it a few times when the Commander was reading and relaxing after lunch. Five hours of work with only chestnut water and a piece of rye bread had brought him to the brink of collapse.

The workers were standing in the foyer about to leave when three golden apples (or was it a mirage?) suddenly rolled along the floor, accompanied by loud laughter. The Commander was amusing himself by kicking the apples as the four workers scrabbled around on their knees trying to seize them. It didn't hurt Daniel's pride to crawl in pursuit of the apple; the humiliation lay in making fun of his hunger. A huge black boot hovered over his hand, threatening it, but then withdrew, kicking the fruit farther away. Daniel was finally able to grab hold of an apple. It wasn't snatched from him, nor were the dogs set loose when he sank his teeth into it. Clearly, the Commander had risen in a good mood. A girl's voice called to him from upstairs. It was no longer a secret: an attractive prostitute must have satisfied him. Perhaps the workers would have two or three calm days. Perhaps.

The afternoon dragged on slowly, despite the memory of the golden apple. That night, after the days spent in the confinement cell, the wooden bunk felt almost soft to Daniel. His fellow in-mates – lice-infested, like him, to a greater or lesser degree – provided a warm, familiar reassurance.

This time they woke him up. He couldn't be allowed to oversleep again. No one would be able to save him then from the terrifying 'aggravating circumstances' and the menacing scrutiny of Dr Rascher. His body still ached from the whipping, but his sleep was deep and free from nightmares – maybe because he felt the comforting presence of those around him.

The barracks 'secretary' roused him from a far different world. In his dreams he had found himself in his orderly workshop, amid the familiar, pleasant smells of wood, glue and varnish – not the fug that permeated the barracks. Upstairs, his mother was humming as she cooked, and the aroma of delicious food filtered down to him. His senses overflowed with well-being: the sun gilded the wood like a warm sunset, like aged gold that had been dyed red – even blue, curiously enough. His collection of steel luthier's knives gleamed with a cold brilliance.

The sweet-smelling wood – beautifully grained plates and flitches – lay ready to be used for violins and violas. Time and air would slowly dry the wood. He had learned from his father to use only wood that had been cut for at least five years. Good mountain spruce and maple, trees where birds had nested and the wind had sung. Where a bow would come to sing. In his dream all the equipment and all the tools sparkled like gems, which in effect they were: the modest jewels of his craftsman's crown. In his dream Daniel was making a viola and had reached one of the most delicate steps: placing the sound post – the *anima* or soul as the Italians called it – the tiny piece of fine-grained spruce that went inside the instrument. He was on the verge of positioning it just beneath the right foot of the bridge, very carefully, absolutely straight, completely vertical. But something was the matter. His hands broke out in a sweat as the sound post slipped out of place. It was too far away, useless now. He would have to begin all over again. But the viola began to fade.

Hands were shaking him, waking him from his dream. The viola had been left soulless. A bad omen, Daniel thought. It wasn't just the dream, however. He didn't have to search far for the bad omen. It lay before him, directly in front of him: dawn. The beginning of a new day at Gehenna, the Three Rivers Camp.

Dark dawn was breaking, like an old blanket thrown across the shabby bed of the suffering, a harbinger of the gray, faltering daylight that awaited them. No nightmare, he thought, could possibly be worse than the cruelty that surrounded them, pervaded them, as inescapable as the air they breathed. He felt powerless, defenseless as a newborn child. He had been consigned into the hands of incomprehensible hatred, forsaken by everyone. Even God.

He had heard his father speak of exiles and pogroms that had occurred during his grandfather's

life, but his own childhood and adolescence had
been peaceful. He recalled his happy Bar Mitzvah
party and his older brother's. The harmony had
been broken only by his father's illness and death.
Perhaps that was why the storm had taken them by
surprise. Engrossed in the work he loved, he had not
noticed the threatening signs and blackening clouds;
they had nothing to do with him or his people, he
thought. When tyranny first made its appearance,
he had worn the yellow Star of David, unaware that
it would become a ticket to death, like the marking
on a tree to be axed. He awoke to the unfamiliar,
brutal reality the day his workshop was looted. Not
far away the venerable neighborhood synagogue was
being consumed by flames. As a child he had often
accompanied his father to celebrations there, and
had always felt protected under the long paternal
prayer shawl, the *tallith*. After that, his people found
themselves more deeply mired in the turbid waters
that were sucking them under.

Daniel had been released from the prison cell two
days before, yet for some reason this day seemed
more interminable than the previous one. A
profound weariness was rising in him, a sense of

impending fatality and desperation. He recognized the signs: he had seen fellow *lager* inmates grow ill, letting themselves sink into death. They now lay beneath the surrounding hills. He was younger than the ones who had embraced death, and he tried to cheer himself, hoped for the strength to continue struggling another day. He felt completely drained when he reached the barracks, and had no wish to talk, only to rest.

The inmates who worked outside of the camp or in the quarries always returned to the barracks later than Daniel, utterly exhausted. A surprise, however, waited for him that night – a glimmer of hope. New slave laborers had arrived to replace the dead. One of the newcomers assigned to the bunk beside him was Freund, a mechanic who had once lived on the same street as Daniel – you could almost have called him a friend. Daniel could read in Freund's eyes the shock and grief he felt upon seeing how gaunt and wasted his old neighbor had grown.

They wept as they embraced each other; tears flowed easily when you were exhausted. As Freund began to talk, Daniel was filled with a sense of joy for the first time at the Three Rivers Camp: Eva was alive and relatively well. Freund had seen her when he was repairing a machine at the Tisch factory, the one that manufactured military uniforms. This was the 'paradise' that had generated the rumors in camp. The news was true: Eva had enough food. All the workers had good rations of rye bread paid for by the factory owner himself, and they often found it coated with margarine, or butter!

The two friends whispered to each other in the dark, Freund plying Daniel with details, trying his best not to dishearten him. At first Eva had been sent to a different camp, one that bore a terrible name; he didn't know how much she had suffered, but she had survived and wasn't far away.

'If I could just escape and see her . . .'

'Don't even give it a thought,' Freund warned. 'It would be your death.'

Daniel had witnessed many summary executions of prisoners after real or supposed escape attempts. The guards were fast with their rifles, and none of them – not any of the Nazis, not the Commander himself – thought twice about shooting prisoners down.

'Hey, how about letting me get some sleep,' an inmate grumbled.

'I'll tell you more tomorrow, if we're still alive,' Freund whispered.

The short conversation left Daniel wide awake. He was not inclined to fantasize, but he couldn't help imagining Eva, seated at the sewing machine, her tiny hands moving the cloth forward, her beautiful legs tirelessly pumping the pedal. More than that, he imagined her plump lips, not pressed against his but open as she licked the creamy butter on the rye bread – thick, heavenly slices that would keep her alive, make her dark eyes sparkle again. He wasn't envious: the vision had assuaged his anguish. The following day he worked hard, filled once again with a desire to live.

The afternoon seemed especially long, the evening endless. He anxiously awaited the arrival of night and more news from his friend. This time they kept their voices lower as they exchanged information about the two families, a long list of obituaries.

'Your little niece, Regina, is safe!'

A German official had helped smuggle children out of the ghetto in clothes boxes, Freund told him, until he was discovered and sent to the Russian Front. As far as he knew, the little girl was at the house of a former client of Daniel's, not a Jew but a kindhearted *goy*, a German from the Sudetenland.

'Yes, of course I know Rudi,' Daniel replied. 'He's married to a distant cousin of mine.'

'They're living outside Krakow,' Freund told him, 'at the grandfather's place, and they've passed her off as their niece. All of them have Aryan documents.'

As the three-year-old niece of a pure Aryan, Regina was the one with the best chance of survival. That is, if the ones posing as her relatives could fatten her up – she'd almost starved in the ghetto.

Maybe she'll be safe, Daniel thought. I'm sure she will be. Lord, how he hoped so!

You could hear the rain outside. Everything would be covered in mud, but it wouldn't be as cold, he thought, as he fell asleep, listening to the metallic clamor of rain pelting the flimsy barracks roof.

III

Such as sit in darkness and in the shadow of death, being
bound in affliction and iron.

– PSALM 107:10

Rascher's refusal to use a woman prisoner of
Nordic appearance in experiments to raise the
body temperature of prisoners frozen in tanks
of ice water – 1943

Four women have been placed at my disposition for use in
raising prisoners' body temperature by means of animal heat;
they were sent from the Ravensbrück concentration camp.

One of these women shows very Nordic racial features:
blond hair, blue eyes, the shape of her head and body.
She is 21 and ¾ years old.

When I objected to the fact that she had volunteered for the brothel, she stated: 'Better to spend six months in the brothel than six months in camp.' She offered strange details about the R. camp, which were confirmed by the other women and the guard who accompanied them.

I find it repugnant to my racial sensitivity that a girl with decidedly Nordic features would offer herself as a prostitute to ethnically inferior prisoners. With the proper assignments, perhaps we can lead her back to the right path. I refuse to use her in experiments for these reasons and address this report to the Commander of the camp and to the assistant to the Reichsführer SS.

– Dr S. Rascher

The greenhouse was finished, as far as Daniel's job was concerned, and the shelf almost filled. Now it was the gardeners' turn to comply with the Commander's whims. Daniel slept very few hours that night, worrying where he would be sent next. It might be the carpenters' shop again; they had chosen him for the job at the Commander's house because of the quality of his carpentry. But he could also be assigned elsewhere, to a place where far greater physical exertion would be required. Everything depended on Sauckel's needs or wishes. From what Daniel had overheard, he believed that new projects were brewing, but there was no telling. Perhaps the Commander was tired of seeing them around his house. The work had been carefully inspected, and apparently they would not be sent to the quarry if the results were deemed satisfactory.

Nothing, however, was mentioned that day, and the four inmates were ordered back to the carpenters' shop. This was fine with Daniel, better to go unnoticed, better not to have your number called. On his way to the workshop, he spotted three prisoners he knew – musicians – all clean and well dressed, heading toward the pavilion, and realized that a party was planned.

Midafternoon, Dr Rascher entered the shop, accompanied by an unfamiliar colleague. The prisoners continued their work as they had been taught to do, never looking up or greeting the officials. Nor did the visitors say anything; they merely observed the men sawing, planing, gluing. But Daniel was nervous. He could feel himself being observed, him alone. He cut his hand but made no sound. The last thing he needed was to injure himself, he thought, as he made an effort to continue working, his eyes fixed on the wood.

Despite the cold, drops of sweat began to accumulate above his forehead, dampening his shaved head. At last, the silent doctors relieved the prisoners of their oppressive company.

They were heading to the Commander's house no doubt, invited to the concert and party. The Monster enjoyed good music and good wine. Occasionally, he even played the violin, and not badly. The musicians had mentioned that he played relatively well, though without much feeling. The party would probably continue until late; some pretty girls would be invited.

Later that afternoon Daniel was absorbed in his work finishing a window frame when a heavy hand touched his shoulder:

'You, over to the Sturmbannführer's place.'

He scurried there as fast as he could, consumed by anxiety. What could the Commander want? Not much apparently: a churlish assistant pointed to a minute defect on one of the doors. Daniel had no trouble repairing it. In the distance he could hear the superb music being played by the trio. Then, suddenly, the Commander shouted. Some strange impulse compelled Daniel to enter the room. The lights, the aroma of delicious food, the smell of tobacco, fear: all of it made him dizzy, and he stopped short for a moment. But he soon realized what had caused the outburst. The problem was the violin in the hands of the fear-blanched musician, Bronislaw, a man he knew well. The young soloist had been well respected before he'd become the object of Sauckel's accusing finger and Rascher's grinning face. But Daniel did not withdraw. No, he would not provide the spectators with cruel amusement. He stood at attention, saluted, and in a thin voice said: 'It's not his fault, sir. The violin has a crack on the top plate. I can fix it.'

The Commander looked at him in astonishment but seemed pleased at the idea that the instrument could be repaired.

A guest with kind eyes, a man Daniel had never seen before, asked him: 'You say you're able to fix it? You mean the violinist wasn't playing badly just to offend our ears?'

As if taking a rose, Daniel gently removed the violin from the hands of the stupefied musician and showed the guest the tiny crack, forgetting for the moment that he was in the house of his enemy. He spoke of his musical vocation in Yiddish sprinkled with German, but with a self-assurance he had not felt for many months, not since he had been reduced to a subhuman prisoner.

Then he stepped back. The conversation between the kind-eyed guest, the Commander and Rascher continued in low voices, too low and too fast for him to understand. The other doctor and the girls said nothing. Daniel had the terrifying feeling that both his future and that of the reprimanded violinist were at stake. A girl poured white wine into everyone's fine crystal glasses. Then Sauckel called an officer over, spoke to him as he pointed to Daniel, and scribbled something on a sheet of paper. He doesn't want to lower himself to speak to me, the luthier thought, but he's made a decision and no doubt I'll be punished again.

The SS officer dragged him from the room without explanation and opened the front door. Daniel rushed down the steps before he could be pushed. Once again he heard laughter and happy voices from the house; the musicians were still in the room. He glanced up, caught sight of the loathsome doctor's face and saw an expression of cold disappointment. A good sign, Daniel thought.

'You made a serious mistake, you bastard.' The officer spat at him once down the steps. 'You

entered the room *and* addressed Herr Sturmbannführer without permission.' After a pause to allow
the gravity of the deed to sink in, he continued,
'Showing great indulgence, he has decided not to
punish you on one condition, that the violin is
repaired by tomorrow morning.'

'But how can I do that, sir?'

Daniel hadn't even noticed that the officer was
carrying the violin!

'Shut up and listen, you idiot! Follow me to the
carpenters' shop, you have all night to work. If the
violin is not to his liking tomorrow, it's confinement with aggravating circumstances for you, plus
whippings before and after confinement. This is
your second offense.'

The officer was panting, as if out of breath
after providing so many details. This was unusual:
punishment was normally meted out with no
explanation. Well, Daniel thought as he was being
accompanied to the workshop, this means no
supper for me. I'll have to manage without, even
though I'm starving. Thank goodness he had
hidden a tiny piece of bread crust in his pocket that
morning; he did this occasionally to help pass a
long afternoon.

The SS officer – still holding the violin – presented the paper to a surly, silent guard, who read it without comment but was clearly even more disgruntled. The officer led Daniel into the shop and handed him the violin. Once the two of them were alone, ignoring regulations, the officer lit a cigarette and blew the smoke in Daniel's face. Seemingly satisfied when Daniel coughed, the officer settled into a chair and kept a sharp eye on the work, visibly skeptical of the luthier's craftsmanship, but he soon stopped smoking and dozed off. The cigarette lay on the floor, snuffed out, but Daniel didn't dare touch it.

He had little company that night: the snores from the guard outside (a common prisoner with a green insignia on his clothes, the kind who's often very cruel) and the occasional screeches of distant night birds down by the broad river beyond the camp, where trees grew, where colors other than gray and white existed. Daniel was familiar with the old name of the river, but not Aqueront, the strange name used by a fellow inmate – a professor from Krakow, imprisoned for being a socialist. The man had been saved from selection because he was listed as a baker. He was in fact the son of a baker and he knew how to knead dough and make bread.

Daniel had to concentrate now on the violin. He hadn't been overly optimistic; his calculations were correct: the crack wasn't deep. The sides could be pressed together, no splinters were showing. Praise God! First, he cast about to see if any of his small carpentry wedges could be used. Fortunately, he always kept the workshop neat. He found two tiny, very smooth cylinders, just the right size – they wouldn't even have to be planed. He didn't have the right violin glue, of course, but he did have a reasonably good one, though lumpy, which he had saved for especially delicate jobs at the Tyrant's pavilion. He lit the little burner and began heating the glue, being very careful not to let it thicken too much.

He was himself once again, not a number, not an object of taunting ridicule. He was Daniel, a luthier by profession. At that moment he thought of nothing other than the job at hand and the pride he took in it. His eyes glistened with precise attention; even his hunger disappeared. With skillful fingers he slowly spread the glue around the crack, all along the edges of it, then forced it well inside. He observed the result with a trained eye and judged it to be good; after all, he had practically been born among violins. The graining matched, which meant that the tiny vertical crack would be well sealed. At least for a while. He located the round cramp in its proper place and set the two wedges beneath it, being careful no glue touched them, then tightened the cramp to the exact size.

Daniel's thoughts wandered as he wiped the sweat from his forehead and examined the work again. He had spilled a drop of glue on the top plate of the violin and couldn't risk letting it dry. He heated some water, in which he dampened a very fine paintbrush and carefully removed the glue. It was a matter of waiting now. It had taken him a long time to perform the delicate task, and he knew the violin wouldn't be dry for at least four hours, probably more with all the humidity. The officer escorting him was still asleep, wrapped in a wool cloak, and Daniel didn't dare wake him for fear of reprisal. Nor could he leave the shop: he knew his furtive shadow would be a sure target for the guard's machine gun. In that case, he thought, trying to comfort himself at the prospect of the dismal night ahead, I'll stand over the violin to be sure nothing happens to it. Too much was at stake.

He was hungry again and noticed that the officer had dropped a piece of apple that had rolled toward him. Using a piece of cloth, Daniel pulled it closer without making a sound and ate it hungrily. He would have to find a way to sleep some, or at least to rest. He warmed his hands at the burner before turning it off and stretched out on the floor, on top of some wood chips that protected him a bit. He tried to sleep but kept waking up. It had stopped raining, and the night was cold and quiet, his dreams anxious. With little conviction he murmured a prayer to his silent God, imploring that his work be approved.

He awoke early and, not wishing to sleep any more, sat down on a stack of wood. He couldn't be late to roll call or skip breakfast. He wasn't scheduled for a shower today, so he washed with a bit of water from the faucet and went outdoors as soon as the siren sounded.

When he returned to the shop, he showed the day guard the paper from the night before, but the guard clearly had already received instructions and muttered: 'Get to work, fast. It's still early; I'll let you know when you have to appear before the Sturmbannführer.'

At least he hadn't hit him. Daniel set about his work, glancing often at *his* violin. A pleasant sensation was mixed with the usual fear when the guard looked at his watch and ordered Daniel to present himself at the Commander's house. Daniel showed the paper and had no trouble getting in. This time Sauckel deigned to speak to Daniel directly, but immediately put him in his place.

'*Ja*, our little carpenter!' he said as he petted his dog.

All the prisoners stooped, but now Daniel instinctively straightened up. He was actually quite tall, but the Commander stood half a span taller. A long moment of uncertainty ensued as the instrument was carefully inspected. He doesn't look like he's in a very good mood, Daniel thought. His forehead's furrowed and wrinkled; maybe he's hungover. The Commander didn't appear very interested in the violin, but he swept his bow across it and played some notes. His forehead cleared, and he smiled.

'All right for now. Back to your shop, and don't let me hear that you aren't hard at work. I'll keep the violin. Out of here.'

Raising his voice, the Commander called out to his aide with cruel amusement: 'I've had the violinist punished. We'll see him when he's out of confinement.'

Then, addressing Daniel again, 'What are you waiting for? Out of my sight.'

Daniel hurried away so fast that he almost fell. His desperate act of courage had not been sufficient to keep the accomplished musician from being punished. Daniel hadn't dared to say a word, not with the Commander standing beside his dog. Who knows, he might have set it loose.

Daniel was miserable when he returned to his carpenter's bench, where fortunately he was never at a loss for work. He had been naïve enough – not yet sufficiently steeped in camp cruelties – to think that the Commander would be satisfied with the newly repaired violin and wouldn't punish Bronislaw, his 'personal' violinist, for something that was not his fault. But logic did not reign at the Dreiflüsselager, much less compassion.

Eva eats good, thick slices of bread and butter, Daniel thought, in an attempt not to let desperation and exhaustion sweep him away. But he immediately returned to his previous train of thought: *I should have warned the Commander that the repair was only provisional, that another, more thorough restoration – opening up the violin, reinforcing it from inside – might be required.* But it had been impossible to utter a word; all his courage had been consumed the night before. Icy fear had sealed his lips. What would happen if the crack reappeared? What would be done to Bronislaw and himself? The thought stayed with him all day as he labored the full eleven and a half hours.

Over his midday soup, Daniel talked to Freund, who was visibly relieved when he saw him. When he hadn't appeared in the barracks the night before, the men there had feared the worst – that he had been sent back to the confinement cell. Daniel had never even given them a thought as he labored over the violin. It wasn't that he had forgotten where he was but that he had moved everything distasteful to a compartment far back in his mind. All of it: the whippings, mud, frost, the damp fog, the shadow of the gallows, the shouts and insults. But it had all resurfaced when Sauckel uttered the words 'I've had the violinist punished.' All the ugliness was snared, like a slimy fish, by the Commander's excruciatingly painful hook.

Bronislaw hadn't been whipped, or at least not in public, or they would have had to form ranks. He might, however, have been whipped in private, in a basement with no one present. It had been done before. If this had happened to Bronislaw, sooner or later it could happen to all of them.

Better not to dwell on it, Daniel thought, but to remember that soon I'll be called back to the Commander's house. The Swine wants yet another shelf . . . maybe the cook will slip me some leftovers. Besides, tomorrow's Thursday, the only day of the week we're given potatoes cooked in their skins, instead of watery turnip soup. Maybe they'll serve me a large potato.

The hours passed slowly, like a long cloak dragging on the ground. The day seemed interminable to Daniel after his sleepless night. It was longer than any other day, except for the four in the confinement cell, where he had lain like a mistreated dog.

That night, murmurs swept through the barracks. The mechanic had more news! But Daniel didn't want to hear, or even know. He was dead tired and could read in the inmates' eyes that the news was bad. He knew it would keep him awake, and he knew that if he did not sleep he would be sick, ready for 'the infirmary' . . . the sinister journey to the Death Camp.

'Tomorrow,' he said. 'Tell me tomorrow.'

The drone of the inmates' whispering rocked him to sleep. There was nothing out there, other than time, other than the river of life, that could not wait. He dreamed he was in an enormous, cold waiting room filled with smoke. Through the window he glimpsed long cattle trains that rolled through the station without stopping, their wagon doors shut. When the doors opened, his friends were shoved onto the platform, but he remained silent, glued to the metal bench where he was sitting. From the ceiling hung corpses and violins. Then a train stopped, but the stationmaster, wearing a military cap and with the same kind eyes as the guest the other night, separated him from the others.

'Not you,' he said. 'This isn't your train. You have to finish the viola.'

An inspector approached, whip in hand, and Daniel wanted to flee. He lifted one leg but couldn't move; he opened his mouth but couldn't scream. He opened it wider and wailed.

'Shut up!' Freund whispered urgently into Daniel's ear, clapping a hand over his mouth. 'You're with me. It's a nightmare.'

* * *

'You were right,' Freund told him at breakfast, his mouth full of bread, 'not to want to know the news last night. You were so upset it would have kept you from sleeping.'

'I feel better this morning, you can tell me.'

All of the inmates had been released after roll call; no incident had occurred. It was 6:15, so the two friends sat down on a rock in the dark while the violin maker listened to the brutal and unwelcome news. By a strange coincidence, perhaps by the will of God or by the Commander's impulsive decision to repair the violin, Daniel had been saved. Now he knew why Rascher had had that expression of disappointment on his face. The luthier was young, still healthy, and no doubt would have made a good specimen. Four young inmates, one of whom was from their barracks, had been 'selected' to participate in the Monster's experiments.

'You didn't even realize last night that one was missing.'

'What'll they do to them?'

Freund was assigned to an auto repair shop, and he often picked up information from reliable sources there. He'd gotten this latest news because the chauffeur for one of the Obersturmführers had been explaining Rascher's projects to another driver.

The horror of the account wormed its way through Daniel, like a snake rising from the mud. Fortunately I'm sitting down, he thought. It can't be true! Could they actually be doing something so horrible? While he had been repairing the crack in the violin and clamping together the beautiful graining, Daniel thought as he covered his mouth to keep from vomiting, the monsters had been plunging prisoners into freezing cold water.

'Four degrees centigrade,' Freund said. 'Very methodical. And they keep them in it till they lose consciousness.'

'Why do they do it? What do they say?'

'The Nazis say it's to apply the results of the experiments to German aviators who are fished from the Baltic when their planes go down, but I don't believe it. Nor do any of the mechanics, not even the officers. I'm sure it's just to see them suffer. It gives them a hard-on to torture people – the bastards – a hard-on stiff as a board.'

'Don't they die from the cold?'

'Some do, but they say it's only a small percentage, "nothing important." You know how they say they bring them back to consciousness? They warm them between two naked women – prostitutes or prisoners. They call it experimenting with animal heat. They watch to see if the prisoners recover, constantly spying on them, taking their temperature. If they regain consciousness, they cover all three of them with a blanket. A mechanic who was at another camp before told me the bastards laughed as they talked about it. But it's time to go now. Come on, get up, make an effort.'

They never saw the inmate from their barracks again.

IV

Mothers' screams mount the silent steps
And the golden hound of dawn seeks their sweet bones.
But they remain below!

– AGUSTÍ BARTRA, *L'arbre de foc*

Report on Security Measures at the Auschwitz Concentration Camp – 1944

Concentration Camp III consists of many isolated subcamps in Upper Silesia that have been established with the object of servicing industrial companies. At the moment of writing, all of these camps have their own security systems, which is to say, they are surrounded by barbed wire, electrified fences and watchtowers.

The subcamps of Concentration Camp III are controlled by 650 brigades of guards.

In order to provide greater security, another measure has been taken: the creation of an exterior security ring controlled by the Wehrmacht. The work camp that services I. G. Farbenindustrie, which currently has at its disposal 7,000 prisoners, lies within this exterior ring. Altogether, the I. G. Farben plants have approximately 15,000 men, in addition to our prisoners.

On the previous day Daniel had glued together the two plates that would form the belly of the violin. The grains from the beautiful Hungarian spruce were a perfect match. He had taken the precaution of slightly warming the edges so the glue would penetrate the pores of the wood. Now came one of the stages that Daniel most enjoyed, although it was one of the most difficult: marking the exact shape he wanted to give the instrument. He had a clear vision in his head, and despite the inevitable obstacles, he was confident that his experience could bring the violin to life.

He couldn't help pausing to smell the wood before he started. He worked for a long time, then stopped when he was tired and looked approvingly at what he had accomplished. The design was exact. He was weak, but his hands had not shaken as he followed the template: the edges were neat, precise. He had probably labored over it too long. He took the fretsaw from its hook, laid it half on, half off the workbench and, uttering a prayer – unconsciously perhaps – he began to saw. For the uninitiated, it can be difficult to maneuver the little saw, never quite touching the outline, leaving only a millimeter to be sanded later, so that the edges will form a clean, clear line, like paper cut with a guillotine. Daniel, however, never found this part difficult. He thought of nothing except the sinuous line he was following, its beautiful shape – just like a woman's body. All of his energy, what little remained, was concentrated in his right hand. He had reclaimed his former talent.

The first half was finished, and his forehead was drenched in sweat from the exertion. He wiped it carefully so it wouldn't affect his vision. He found the second part less tiring. As the silhouette of the violin began to acquire the shape of the template, drawing closer to his mind's ideal, he was filled with a sense of well-being – something he hadn't experienced for months – a physical well-being even. His hands possessed a memory of their own, he knew they did. The musicians who trusted him to repair their violins or cellos, or commissioned a new viola, had said the same. Daniel had always enjoyed talking to them, learning new things about their profession. His luthier fingers had guarded the memory of the delicate tasks demanded by his craft.

No, this time he didn't wake up with a start, nor did anyone have to shake him out of his slumber. His mornings were spent crafting the violin. But the mealtime siren, the hurried departure of carpenters and cabinetmakers anxious to finish their shift, the sudden hunger pains reminded him that this was not *his* shop. He was in the *lager*, ordered by the Commander to make a violin.

All of the workshops within the camp, except for the ones that repaired vehicles, were now closed in the afternoons. All capable prisoners were employed in the plants that manufactured airplane and tank parts, weapons. The bombings were constant, and some of the prisoners had been put to work constructing underground galleries for a new arms factory. Daniel was sent to one of the I. G. Farben factories, one of many that exploited slave labor. Freund, however, remained in the camp working in the repair shop all day; the Führers and chauffeurs continued to value him because he was an exceptionally good mechanic.

At his carpenter's bench, Daniel felt alive again, but when he and his co-workers left at the end of the shift, he had the impression that he was entering a nightmare where he was caught in a monster's slimy tentacles. Rather than a nocturnal nightmare, this one commenced at midday; the semblance of calm acquired during the morning vanished, and in its place a knot gripped his chest. The whole idea of *his* violin seemed absurd, like a rose in a pigsty. A violin in the Three Rivers Camp. A violin as a survival tactic. Perhaps.

Unexpected events, unpleasant ones usually, surprised him but little; he had slowly become inured to them. Anything could happen. The crowded barracks could grow more crowded, additional bunks could be squeezed in for new prisoners – some of whom were always Russian. Inmates could be deprived of lunch with the excuse that they hadn't worked hard enough at the factory. Or, on the contrary, they could discover that a raw carrot had been added to the turnip soup, following the new doctor's advice (Rascher had been promoted).

They could be ordered on a Tuesday or Friday morning to stand in formation in the Appellplatz – near the site where Daniel had been whipped – and, stiff and trembling from the cold, witness the hanging of a 'subversive' prisoner accused of being a spy or a communist.

Although everything in the camp had come to seem equally illogical, equally quotidian, still Daniel had been astonished when he was suddenly ordered to make a violin: as well crafted 'as if it were a Stradivarius,' the Untersturmführer had demanded. Even more astonishing were the tools, wood and articles placed at his disposal. He thought at the time that the material must have been confiscated from the workshop of a Jewish luthier, German maybe, someone who might be dead, murdered. He didn't recognize any of the material as coming from his own workshop in Krakow. It was a direct order from the Sturmbannführer, he was told, and he was forbidden to ask any questions, even if he meticulously adhered to formality.

'Number 389 respectfully requests permission to ask a question, sir,' he had stated after standing at attention and saluting.

'Permission denied.'

At least the words were not accompanied by a kick. The extended arm pointed toward the door to the carpenters' shop. Daniel needed no urging; he entered immediately and was assigned a section of the room for him alone.

He labored in silence, closely scrutinized by a Ukrainian kapo, trying his best not to ponder the reasons that lay behind the violin, much less to comment on the work with his fellow inmates – he didn't want to create any ill will. Daniel thought he might be able to glean some information from the Commander, but no opportunity presented itself.

Work advanced slowly the first days. Before he could even commence, he had to organize the confiscated material, select the wood he wanted, remove the chips adhered to it. Progress was also hindered because he was accustomed to *his* luthier knives, *his* gouge, plane, pliers. His own tools were wedded, so to speak, to the shape of his hands, all of them shiny and clean in his ground-floor workshop. Where had it all gone: the quiet, pleasant neatness of his workshop, the rows of violins hanging from the ceiling, the familiar warmth, his mother's voice singing softly upstairs as she worked – his mother, who had died in the ghetto of tuberculosis or hunger.

He had not even been allowed to ask how long he had to finish the violin without being punished. He noticed, however, that after he had worked for several days, no one bothered him. The guard no longer beat him, he hadn't been sent back to the confinement cell, Rascher hadn't reappeared. He was whipped again one morning – everyone in the barracks was when officials discovered two hidden apples – but he was immediately sent back to work. As he labored over the violin, he began to grow more confident, despite the fact that morning was divorced from afternoon, as if the day were split in two by a sword. Daniel never found it difficult to become absorbed in his work or to store away in the attic of his brain all the fury and fog that surrounded him. That is, as long as no particular 'incident' occurred during roll call, no dogs sank their teeth into a prisoner's leg because of some innocent or suspicious movement, and only the usual insults were dispensed. Sometimes the fragment of a melody sprang to his lips, dying before it could find a voice, or snatches of old prayers hidden in the folds of his memory – *Jevarehehà Adonài*.

As he stood in line for his midday soup, Daniel was thinking that, despite the gnawing in his stomach, he felt almost happy while he labored over the belly of the violin. But – as was the case with most of the inmates – hunger evoked memories, fantasies of past meals. If he was forced to wait longer than usual, visions emerged of a well-laid table and the delicious kosher food his mother cooked. He would imagine the two holiday meals at Passover with all the relatives, uncles and cousins. The basket with the *haroseth*, the bitter herbs that would have tasted so good now, the hard-boiled eggs, the white silk cloth with blue stripes that covered them ... What he would have given for a hard-boiled egg today! Or better still, a piece of lamb. He remembered the taste of the matzo – the unleavened bread – and the fun of searching for the hidden piece, the prize for the child who found it. He didn't want to think about the songs or the three toasts. If he could just have a few spoonfuls of *cholent* – the terrine of rice, eggs, dried beans and goose that had to be cooked all night in the community oven. As a young boy, he'd been sent more than once to fetch it.

His vision vanished cruelly when he was handed the soup, the same soup as every day, except Thursdays, when the potatoes were a bit more filling. He knew what awaited him. The five or six hours at the factory that afternoon with nothing in his stomach other than the watery soup would drive him, as it did every day, to the brink of exhaustion and desperation. He often thought that he wouldn't be able to make the effort to rise the following morning. His day had come to resemble a face that has suffered an accident: beautiful on one side, burnt or scarred on the other.

He wasn't always able to devote the entire morning to the violin; sometimes instruments were brought to him for repair. Strange as it may seem, the enemy had assembled a small orchestra in the camp, as they had in others. It had taken Daniel a long time to organize all the material he had been given. The day after it arrived he had been asked to choose the pieces he needed and set aside those he didn't. He suspected that what he discarded would be sold. He was careful, in any case, to ensure that he would have extra wood and rough flitches in the event a plate cracked, or he needed to repair an instrument. He discovered a few ready-cut pieces of beautiful spruce and maple and some ebony end buttons. He kept two of the violin bows – one needed repairing, but the other looked brand new – some braided strings, also some sycamore and ebony for the purfling. He set aside a number of strips of wood that had been cut for ribs and kept all of the tools – he would need every one of them. He was relieved to find three sound posts that had already been crafted (better to have too many). They would likely save him some work. The jars and boxes with different kinds of gum and glue – liquid and granulated – kept him occupied for some time, but now they stood in a neat row, the name clearly marked on each. In the end, he discarded very little, but fortunately no one rebuked him. Daniel determined that all of the material must have come from the workshop of an excellent craftsman.

In the afternoon, he found it difficult to concentrate on the boring factory work. That morning he had finally been able to finish the top plate of the violin, and it was ready to be planed. He was becoming obsessed with his instrument. But he couldn't let his mind wander, in part to keep from being reprimanded, in part to maintain the proper pace, to neither interfere with nor accelerate the work in his sector. The kapo – also a Ukrainian prisoner – wasn't one of the cruelest, but when it was in his interest, he demanded that the established quota be met.

From time to time Sauckel himself or another commander made an appearance, and their visits rarely ended well. One terminated with the death of a prisoner accused of sabotage. Daniel always suspected that one of the men in his sector had pointed his finger at the disagreeable fitter – otherwise, why would they have gone straight to him? The officials didn't want the commotion of a public execution, perhaps to avoid betraying the informer. The Commander rebuked the fitter and shouted an order at two of his aides, who then dragged the prisoner outside. No one ever saw him again.

In some cases when the prisoners hadn't accomplished the assigned task, they were forced to begin half an hour earlier the following day and weren't given any lunch. For all of these reasons, Daniel made an effort to work hard, always careful not to scrape his hands, so as not to affect his ability to craft the violin. He forced himself to wait until nighttime to think about his precious instrument.

Having been absorbed in his violin for so many weeks, he had only now realized that the days were less short, less cold; it was no longer dark when the prisoners assembled for the morning roll call. The dawn light now revealed the scandalous marks

of their long slavery: Daniel could see the gaunt
faces of the rows of men dressed in shabby clothes
that bore the sinister colored rectangles – yellow
ones, primarily – dark circles under their eyes, the
signs of beatings and scars on some faces. Had he
lost count of the time? The days were like years, the
months like days, all of it muddled indistin-
guishably together.

Nothing existed other than the camp, other
than this island, this monstrous archipelago of
subcamps. He felt a gust of wind, and the air was
less icy, more gentle. It was the first benevolent
gesture in this land of hatred. The swallows would
be nesting soon on the street where he had lived in
Krakow. Spring, he told himself, would bloom
brighter than ever. It would bloom over the bodies
of the thousands of dead. It wasn't a comforting
thought, but it was true.

He found the coffee more bitter, the slice of
bread punier, almost as if his thoughts had weighed
it down, kept it from rising. A few moments later,
as the inmates were heading to their work areas, he
paused to glance at the sky – something he rarely
did because he found it always shrouded in clouds
or fog – and discovered large patches of blue. A

harsh slap on his back forced him to march again. Yes, he thought again as he stifled a sob, spring is drawing near. Our dead will fertilize the earth and spring will return.

With this in mind, his shoulder still aching, Daniel trudged through the door of the carpenters' shop. He shrugged the thought off and began to polish the edges of the top plate for the last time. He sniffed the wood as he picked up the mold that would cradle the belly and, using the tiny gouge, began to remove the extra wood from inside the plate. This required an art as subtle as that of the poets. The slap, the reminder of death, the expectation of long hours at the factory all vanished, as if the smell of the wood were a breeze that swept away the dark, threatening clouds. The guard who was watching him was distracted as he ate his lunch, and Daniel was able to rest a moment without endangering himself. He placed the minute finger planes – three different sizes – within arm's reach so they would be ready for gouging the wood down to the appropriate delicate thickness.

After considerable thought, he had decided to leave the central part of the belly four and a half millimeters thick. He usually left it at five, but he had been ordered to craft an instrument 'like the Stradivarius'; the edges he would plane down to three millimeters. Working under less than ideal conditions, he didn't want to risk making the plates any thinner, but the sound would be full if he crafted the instrument in this manner, following the dictates of the school founded by Mateusz Dobrucki, who had been, like himself, a Krakow man. Daniel despised violins and violas with walls too thick, their sound flat and lifeless. He moved the gouge confidently, going against the grain of the wood, as his father – Peace be upon him – had taught him. Not a single long shaving appeared, as it should be. After all, he'd been in the profession since he was fourteen!

Daniel continued his work, surrounded by the smell of wood chips, the sounds of planing, the occasional hammer stroke. He stopped for a moment and checked the thickness again, clearly pleased with his skill. He had reached six millimeters. It was time to switch to the finger plane, which would help his task considerably; he had never had any problem planing the arches.

The days were growing brighter. Judging by the light and the amount of work he had accomplished, Daniel calculated that it was almost noon. As he was thinking this, he heard the door of the workshop abruptly swing open. He didn't turn around. Whoever it was – inspectors or visitors – it was essential that they find the inmates absorbed in their tasks. Suddenly Daniel's plane refused to budge. He didn't look up, he didn't have to. Please, God, keep me from being paralyzed, don't let me ruin the violin, he implored. Above the usual din of the workshop – sounds he always enjoyed – he recognized two unmistakable voices, branded into his brain by fear. The louder, deeper voice belonged to Sauckel, the other to Rascher.

Daniel felt as if everyone could hear his heart pounding, but his mind worked fast. The two men were standing near the other prisoners, some distance from his section of the shop. He gently placed the belly of the violin on the table he used for the most delicate tasks, strolled over to his carpenter's bench and picked up the piece of maple that he had cut to size for the neck of the violin. Admiring the beautiful flames that ran the length of the wood, he began to plane one edge. It had occurred to him in a flash that he could do this job by instinct, even with Rascher's cold eyes fixed on him. The rhythm of the plane calmed him. Then the two men stood before him.

'How is the violin coming along?'

To his surprise, the Commander's voice showed no ridicule or insult. It seemed to express the natural curiosity of a client. Daniel managed to respond with a clear voice: 'It's going quite well, sir, without a problem.'

He continued to work as he spoke. He had learned always to question official reactions. He had been thrashed for not standing at attention when addressed; he had been thrashed when he stopped work to stand at attention. There was no thrashing this time. As he planed, he could see the men out of the corner of his eye. They watched with curiosity when Daniel picked up the carpenter's square and ruler to measure the exact size of the neck. They seemed pleased with the beautiful grain of the wood. Aren't these bastards ever going to leave? Daniel wondered.

Daniel was a skilled craftsman and worked fast. He was ready now to scribe the pattern for the neck, the rounded head, everything that had to be marked – including the holes to indicate the shape the spiral would take, the elegant curve of the scroll. He could not do it calmly with those four eyes trained on his hands. Finally, he heard the visitors depart, and an almost violent sense of relief raced through his body, like a fever leaving a sick man. The excruciating tension began to subside, and he placed the neck of the violin on the workbench and wiped the sweat from his brow.

As he walked back to his worktable, Daniel's knees buckled, and he realized how great his fear had been. He ran his tongue over his lips; they were dry, his throat too. He leaned briefly against the bench and took a deep breath. He needed air but didn't want to ask permission to step outside; he might run across the two officers. Their visit had seemed so long that he calculated it was almost time for the midday siren. He needed to get back to work; it wouldn't do to attract the guard's attention by resting too long.

Daniel concluded that the visit hadn't brought any particularly bad consequences; nobody in the workshop had been hit or punished. The thought helped calm him. He was less agitated when he picked up the compass and the tiny millimeter tape to measure the thickness of the arch. After that, he continued working with the smallest of the planes.

Fortunately, Father – May his memory be for a blessing – taught me well! Daniel thought. He gazed with satisfaction at the morning's work, the results of an eventful session. The following morning he would begin by reinforcing the joints of the two plates with tiny, paper-thin wedges; then he would burnish the inside with sandpaper so the edges would be rounded.

He rubbed his hand along the smooth arch inside the belly of the violin; he trusted his sense of touch as much as he did the compass. He had never believed that any tool could be more precise than his fingertips. He noticed with justified apprehension that they were growing coarse, losing their sensitivity from working in the factory; he sensed the beginnings of a troublesome roughness. But not even this could discourage him as he caressed the two pieces of wood that formed the belly, recalling as he did how desperately he had held Eva during the incursions into the ghetto. The siren sounded abruptly, announcing the end of the shift.

Daniel realized that the inspection had not gone as well in other workshops. He caught sight of one of the Führers, followed by two kapos with a prisoner between them. A strange silence reigned in the camp, broken only by frightened murmurs as the inmates watched the prisoner being locked in a dark cell. The hunting expeditions never ended until the heroes had captured someone in their snares.

V

Ah, our musicians' hands have been severed, our singers'
mouths barred with iron.
The sweet-voiced violin lies on the ground.

— YANNIS RITSOS

Inventory of Clothes and Other Objects Collected
at the Lublin and Auschwitz Concentration
Camps, Addressed to the Reich Minister of
Economy (Fragment)

Men's clothing, used
    (not counting white clothing)   *97,000 items*
Women's clothing, used (idem)   *76,000 items*
Women's silk underwear   *89,000 items*
Total number of wagons   *34*

Cloth:	*400 wagons, equivalent to 2,700,000 kilos*
Eiderdown feathers:	
	130 wagons, equivalent to 270,000 kilos
Women's hair:	*1 wagon, equivalent to 3,000 kilos*
Old material:	*5 wagons . . .*

Total	*2,973,000 kilos*
	536 wagons

Total wagons	*570 wagons*

In exchange for a small bribe of cigarettes, the new, more venal kapo cautiously handed Daniel a jar of ointment that would – Daniel hoped – heal his hands. Freund had collected the cigarettes with relative ease from the chauffeurs at the vehicle repair shop, and the luthier had saved them, one by one, until he had enough. On the long day of the Commander and Rascher's visit, exactly two weeks before, all the prisoners had been given a medical examination, perhaps a consequence of orders sent from higher up, by the cold-eyed doctor himself. The various Führers in charge of the camp – Freund always referred to them as Pigs – had baptized the medical routine with the name Spring Cleaning, perhaps because winter had taken its toll on the weak, had killed so many of them, thus sparing officials some of their work.

Daniel lay in his bunk that night, spreading a thick layer of ointment on his hands, thinking himself fortunate to have passed the checkup. This time it hadn't been just the usual rapid once-over that was mandatory before a prisoner was whipped. The camp was small; it had been possible to examine all of the prisoners on the same day. Like the others, Daniel had stood naked as a skinned rabbit; he had been weighed, groped, obliged to bend over, his chest sounded. Finally, he had been considered fit for work rather than the slaughter-house, the black-smoke Death Camp.

The 'healthy' ones were shut in the barracks earlier than usual that night. Daniel lay awake until late – his fellow inmates asleep or pretending to sleep so they wouldn't have to discuss the horrors of the selection. He thought he heard the sound of trucks returning, but it was too early! They must not have taken the others to another *lager*; they hadn't had enough time to go to Auschwitz-Birkenau and back. The frail, sick prisoners must already be dead and buried – stripped of clothing, no shrouds, no farewells, lying in a clearing in the forest close to the Three Rivers Camp. The desperate shouts that had punctured the night, piercing the flimsy wooden walls, were proof that few had believed the story that they would be transferred to a hospital, not even when they were ordered to put their clothes on again. Daniel wanted to recite the prayer for the dead, but he couldn't: the world had turned to ice when he witnessed the children selected to die. He shook Freund, who appeared to be sleeping.

'Do you hear the sound of engines? It's the trucks, isn't it?'

'Yes,' Freund confirmed in a wide-awake voice. 'They were in a hurry! You didn't wake me, I couldn't sleep. The murdering bastards didn't shoot them. I started to suspect what they'd do when they brought us two Saurer trucks to be repaired – faulty brakes. Damn them all, me too; I was forced to help with the repair.' His voice broke as he stifled a sob.

Daniel didn't require more explanation, nor did words exist to console his friend. The two of them lay in silence. The rumor circulating through camp about the death trucks was true; no one knew how it started, but it had spread like an epidemic.

So that was why the trucks broke down so often. They left the main highway and traveled over rough, muddy roads, never stopping because to do so might provoke a rebellion or escape attempts. Crushed together inside the truck, the prisoners were caught in a deadly mousetrap, their illnesses quickly cured when the driver – whose services were paid for with a double ration of alcohol – pulled the lever and they breathed the fumes from the diesel engine. The children too were released from the insidious snares of their childhood. Daniel would have smashed his hands in rage, but he couldn't allow himself even that senseless gesture if he wanted to survive.

He felt as if he had just fallen asleep when the siren sounded, announcing that, despite everything, a new day was commencing. Roll call was shorter that morning, and some of the prisoners were counting their dead. The sun began shamelessly to unravel the fog, banishing it from the sky, and the names of the murdered were swept away by the wind, removed to nothingness.

Not everyone had forgotten them. The implacable camp organization that imprisoned and decimated them still functioned; the officials had taken careful count of the dead, and the report was filed. The prisoners confirmed that no extra slices of bread were available, and, as always, the coffee was thin as a fleeting thought. New lists were quickly drawn up, even as the camp awaited other ill-fated prisoners to fill the cavities left in bunks, in workshops, at roll call. Not all of those who were expected would finally arrive; news had reached the *lager* that many had chosen the path of rebellion or death and were fighting in the Warsaw ghetto.

With the same empty feeling in his stomach as every morning, but accompanied now by a deep bitterness, Freund returned to the repair shop, grumbling to himself, anticipating more work than ever. Daniel too was more despondent than usual as he entered his shop. He had lost his best co-worker, a carpenter who had been coughing for days. He was unable to throw off the deep oppression that gripped his chest. No relief came from glancing at *his* tools, at *his* violin that was now beginning to take shape. He felt his arms less strong, his hands more slow. Somehow I have to purge yesterday's memories, he thought. I can't allow myself the time to remember those who are no longer with us – unless I wish to join their company beneath the birch trees.

Little by little, he went through the motions of his usual tasks. Breathing in the fragrance of the wood, he regained a certain serenity, and the asphyxiating knot of remembrance was loosened. The previous day's physical exertion, the thirty exercises, hadn't been overly strenuous, but it had taken its toll on his weak body. His knees still hurt. The recent unexpected cold, the wind blowing from Russia, the long roll calls, had left his hands lacerated. But the ointment must be doing the trick, he thought; his hands were definitely better today, and that was essential for his work.

At present he lived with what he considered a reasonable expectation: that they would allow him to survive at least until the instrument was finished. He had learned that the Commander collected violins, so surely they wouldn't send him to the quarry now that his specially crafted violin was partially completed. This was something exceptional for the camp, and Daniel found it flattering; it gave him a sense of pride. But he had to maintain his usual pace; if the idea ever crossed the Commander's mind that he was dragging his feet, he would be whipped for working slowly – or for sabotage. Even Freund, whose work seemed indispensable to the camp, had been locked up for a week when he broke one of his tools!

Daniel attempted to maintain the same rhythm he had during the happy years in his own shop in Krakow. It was a miracle that he had been able to finish the belly and the beautiful neck of the violin. He was now carefully, very precisely, setting the bass bar. He wanted to finish that part this morning, so that he could relax on Sunday afternoon and wash some of his clothes. It was the only restful moment he had during the week. He checked the graining on the strip of spruce and set the bass bar so that the grain coincided exactly with that of the belly. He checked the position, assuring himself that it was slightly slanted and running in the same direction the strings would. He held the pieces up to look at them against the light, to be certain that the bass bar fit exactly into the contours of the arching. He knew now how he needed to glue it, where to put more pressure. He had at hand the felt-covered wooden tongs he would use to adjust the piece once it was glued. When the five clamps were in place, he allowed himself to rest a moment while the glue dried. He had removed the excess glue, but it was too late to begin working on a new piece.

The guard had constantly thrashed Daniel during his first few weeks in camp, but now he left him pretty much alone. The guard had even stopped insulting him and seemed satisfied with the luthier who labored in silence, rarely asked permission to use the latrine, didn't cause problems or speak to other carpenters. Even so, it was better not to press his luck: Daniel decided to keep his hand on the violin top to give the appearance of working, but he was careful not to apply any pressure. He sat down on the stool he had made but continued to act as if it were necessary to hold the violin.

Not wanting to remember the terrible selection of the previous day, he tried to direct his thoughts – as if guiding a compliant tool – toward his niece Regina, the little blue-eyed doll he had held so often. His arms were strong then; he used to toss the laughing child high in the air and catch her. It comforted him to believe her safe, though he had had no further news of her. The family would never endanger themselves by contacting him. His cousin, of almost Aryan descent, had two sons who were adolescents now; they probably all doted on the little girl. He recalled that the grandfather kept bees and had a little vegetable garden, so they must have enough food. Surely, the dark circles and sunken eyes, the signs of hunger that had marked her cheeks, would have disappeared by now.

It was better not to think about the dead, but about Regina, and Eva, who was safe at the Tisch factory. Thank goodness his work could still calm him, but he had noticed that he was growing weaker, less sturdy. He could breathe more easily today, was grateful for the sympathetic sun that filtered through the transparent paper affixed to the paneless window. The guard was sitting at a distance, not watching, munching on a handful of nuts he'd managed to find, waiting for his midday meal. How Daniel longed for the almonds the guard was loudly crunching, probably on purpose to make the others envious. At least the guard was distracted; it allowed the prisoners a moment of rest and calm.

Daniel was fortunate, extremely fortunate. The carpenter whose bench was closest to his had slipped over to Daniel's spot to wake him up. Daniel had never fallen asleep at work before, but he had hardly slept the previous night after the trucks returned. He was so exhausted that morning that he had rested his head on the bench, beside the violin, and had fallen asleep. Thank goodness no one else had noticed, or at least none of the other workers had ratted on him to the kapo, as they sometimes did to earn points.

I can never let this happen again, Daniel thought. He had learned in the last few days just how much could be at stake. He'd heard it from Bronislaw, the violinist who had befriended him after Daniel had tried to save him from being punished – as if both of them were not equally defenseless, equally unarmed. Bronislaw had been arrested, but he had been able to avoid the whippings and the Spring Cleaning. He had been assigned to work all day in the kitchen, except on the occasions when the Commander sent for him to play in the trio or the orchestra. Bronislaw's well-trained ear caught every snatch of enemy conversation. It seemed that both men owed their lives to the kind-eyed guest, a friend of Tisch's, a man by the name of Schindler, a benevolent *goy*. Unfortunately, the man had left and hadn't returned, and his factory was far from there. In the meantime, although Rascher had been assigned to another *lager*, he was a frequent, more ominous visitor. The doctor had been heard bragging about the fact that Himmler, the SS Reichsführer, the Great Swine himself, had congratulated him on his terrible experiments with freezing prisoners.

'Just be really careful that the violin is perfect,' Bronislaw had said. 'I know you will. Sauckel seems especially interested in having it turn out well; he's been collecting musical instruments for some time. Wonder how many he's stolen? But as far as yours goes, he's placed a bet with the fanatical Rascher, a whole case of Burgundy wine.'

'You sure you got that right?'

'Not all the details. You know they don't like us to get very close, but what I understood was, if you finish it in the time they agreed on – I couldn't hear how long – and the tonal quality is good, the doctor will have to give the Commander a case of Burgundy wine.'

Bronislaw was silent for a few moments then continued reluctantly, 'The problem is Rascher doesn't particularly like wine; he's more of a beer drinker.'

'What's that supposed to mean?'

Bronislaw wasn't sure; he had his suspicions, but he didn't want to divulge them. Daniel had to force it out of him, almost prying the words from him with his pliers. The doctor didn't want 'things'; he wanted people, bodies, as he had already demonstrated. Bronislaw feared that the value Rascher had assigned to the bet was the luthier himself. A case of wine against Daniel, who – if the bet were lost – would be delivered to the sadistic doctor.

If you thought about it from the Nazis' point of view, it was a high price for one of the Untermenschen, the subhumans.

VI

Pain – has an Element of Blank –

– EMILY DICKINSON

Letter Addressed to Himmler Concerning the Use
of Deceased Prisoners' Gold Teeth – 1942

Economic and Administrative Main Office
Noted in book no. 892/ secr. 42

To the SS Reichsführer,
Reichsführer!
All pieces of dental gold from deceased prisoners will
be delivered to the Health Department according to your
orders. They can be used for dental operations required by
our men.

SS Oberführer Blaschke now has 50 kilos of gold at his disposal, which is the amount of precious metal that will be needed for the next five years.

I request permission, on receiving your authorization, to begin depositing in the Reich Bank all gold dental pieces taken from deceased prisoners in the various concentration camps.

Heil Hitler!

Frank

SS Brigadenführer, Major General of the Waffen-SS

Fragment from the Nuremberg Trials Concerning the I. G. Farben Case

The outrage inflicted on the prisoners by the kapos was terrible. They behaved in an inhuman fashion. I was informed by Walther Dürrfeld or by Engineer Faust that some of the prisoners were shot when they attempted to escape.

I was aware that prisoners were not paid. Around 1943, I. G. Farben introduced a system of awards for the prisoners, which was meant to provide them the opportunity to buy things at the canteen and, at the same time, raise their productivity.

The total amount paid to prisoners over a period of two and a half years came to 20 million marks, which we delivered to the SS.

Daniel froze when he heard the words tumble, in fits and starts, from the musician's mouth. He was paralyzed, speechless, as he tried to understand. He gulped, swallowing saliva as if it were bitter medicine, and said: 'They won't take me alive.'

Daniel let out a yell, causing several prisoners to turn around. Before he could scream again and draw the kapo's attention, Bronislaw clamped his hand over Daniel's mouth, then embraced him, letting his friend's face rest against his threadbare sweater. For months Daniel had lived with incredible tension, and Bronislaw believed that only a much louder scream, a wild, savage wail, would calm him. But protest wasn't possible. The present anguish could only be partially assuaged in the arms of a friend, away from those who would look at Daniel with scorn or wish to add to his anxiety.

After what seemed like a long time to both of them, Daniel broke loose and Bronislaw suggested that walking would calm them. As they strode,

Daniel concentrated, dry-eyed, on what his friend had to say.

'Listen,' Bronislaw said soothingly. 'You won't be removed. The factories can't afford to lose any men. Things are starting to look bad for these wretched murderers. You'll manage, you know you will. The violist from the orchestra where I used to play told me you were tremendously skillful. You did great work for him.'

Bronislaw spoke with conviction, easing Daniel's fears. The luthier wanted to believe his friend's words. He had no other choice.

'Your violin will produce the most beautiful sound imaginable, and I'll see to it that I'm the one to play it. We can do this, we will.'

His friend's voice was like salve applied to an open wound. When he was again reasonably serene, they began to discuss the matter in an almost objective fashion: the difficulty didn't reside in the quality of the work – Daniel wasn't at all anxious about that. Both of them agreed that the problem lay in not knowing the time limit. No one could clarify this; no one wanted to. The musician couldn't ask anyone, nor could he show, even intimate, that he knew about the appalling bet. The consequences could be terrible, and Bronislaw recognized that he was not that brave a man.

It was almost certain – to the degree that one could be certain of anything in this Empire of Terror – that they would allow the luthier to live in Dreiflüsselager until the violin was finished. He wouldn't be moved to the main Auschwitz camp or to Plaszow. His mornings would be spent plying his trade. This was no small privilege in a labor camp; most prisoners had far less. Bronislaw and Daniel agreed not to discuss the matter with anyone, not with the mechanic who had become such a close friend – he was too talkative – nor with the other two musicians. Bronislaw advised Daniel not to rush making the violin, even if he was tempted. It would be much worse if he injured his hands or damaged the instrument. Everything would be lost if the violin didn't produce the proper sound. Bronislaw was convinced that if the violin turned out well – as they had every reason to expect – the Commander would not surrender Daniel to the doctor. There were many other camps, many other victims. After all, the Commander was the boss in his *lager*.

'And he's a rank higher than Rascher,' the musician continued.

Bronislaw had discovered this when he heard them saluting each other, and he knew for a fact that the Commander didn't like to have his authority disputed. One more factor weighed in Daniel's favor: the doctor didn't know a thing about violins, but Sauckel did, and he was astute enough to have set a time limit that wouldn't cause suspicion and would procure him a case of Burgundy wine. Of that Bronislaw was sure!

'So how do you find time to practice?' Daniel asked.

'It's a real problem, since I work in the kitchen all day. Look at my hands! At least they're warm, but I'm worried about the summer.'

Bronislaw managed to practice with the other two musicians in the short period after supper and before the barracks were locked. 'It's not much, but we make an effort "to keep our fingers,"' he explained. 'Look, today we'll barely have half an hour, so I have to leave you now.'

Bronislaw departed reluctantly, walking slowly, unsteadily. Daniel's eyes were full of gratitude as they followed him as far as the barracks. The musician had understood Daniel, comforted him. Fortunately, the two friends had been able to discuss the ghastly problem in all of its details because the days were longer now that it was spring and prisoners didn't have to be back in the barracks until nine.

The luthier left the conversation feeling calmer and fell asleep that night expecting to be able to finish the violin, and freshly determined to do so. For that reason Daniel wasn't particularly alarmed when an unfamiliar kapo showed up at his shop two or three days later looking for him. He figured it was to take him to the Commander's house. He had almost decided, as he was putting away his tools, that he'd ask how much time he had to make the violin. I'll ask him, he thought, in a way that he'll never suspect a thing, as if I believe the Commander needs the violin for a concert. But the kapo had come for a different reason.

'To the clothing workshop, you and the cabinetmaker, and fast,' he ordered. But when Daniel didn't budge, he gave him a shove and yelled, '*Schnell, schnell!*'

Daniel was nervous as he followed the kapo. He needed all the time he had to craft the violin; if he was deprived of any of it, he'd never be able to finish. What could they want with him at the clothing workshop? He didn't know how to iron or sew like a tailor. The only thing that occurred to him was that they might want him to wash the dead prisoners' clothes; they were always reused.

It had been months since Daniel had seen a robust, attractive woman up close, and he found himself fascinated by the body of the baton-wielding SS woman. She was guarding a group of pale, thin women and girls who were sorting and ironing a pile of clean clothes. With a quick glance, Daniel realized some were children's clothes, from the few children who had been living in the camp before the selection. The clothes that were too ragged and couldn't be mended had been placed in a separate pile, probably to make paper pulp. Daniel was well aware that everything in the camp, even old teeth, was put to some use.

The group of 'healthy' prisoners hadn't had their teeth examined, but he had spotted the line of sickly prisoners being examined by a dentist with a brush and a can of paint on his desk. After the Spring Cleaning the prisoners had learned that tongues of paint had marked the naked bodies of prisoners with gold teeth.

Daniel had not been summoned to wash

clothes. He, the cabinetmaker and two other prisoners were escorted to a squat, skillful tailor who measured them and had them try on some reasonably new clothes. The guard was told to bring them back the following day for another fitting. Then the men were taken away. It wasn't that he didn't need new garments. The ones they wore – all the prisoners – were so threadbare that they hadn't protected them from the cold that winter, and pneumonia had ravaged the prisoners. But why would their captors bother to give the men decent sets of clothes?

The four of them talked it over as they left the tailor, but none could figure it out. One of the men had noticed that the jacket he tried on was thicker, well lined, and suggested that maybe they would be sent to a colder camp, farther north. But that was absurd; the Nazis never worried about their health! Daniel brushed the matter aside, having no desire to rack his brains for an explanation, and he and the cabinetmaker returned to the carpenters' shop.

On the following day, in the faltering light of early morning, new suits were distributed to Daniel and the others and a few alterations made. They were issued shoes, and as they were putting them

on, one of the most feared, most cruel Untersturm-
führers stormed in, accompanied by an SS girl with
a camera. The prisoners were warned to obey orders
without asking any questions. One order, however,
proved difficult to follow. Once they were dressed
according to SS tastes and their faces made up,
they were instructed to smile and pretend to be
freely working!

'Unless you wish to see the potatoes growing
above you.'

That was the standard phrase to refer to the
dead. The SS obviously wanted photographs for
propaganda. They had even made a false documen-
tary: *Camp Inmates Working Happily* or *Each Man
With a Job He Enjoys*. A wave of rage surged through
Daniel's body, turning his face scarlet beneath the
makeup. The SS officer grinned and waved his
baton: before it could strike, the prisoners smiled.
If you could call it a smile: their lips separated, their
fear-stricken eyes wide open. While the prisoners
staved off the blows by means of the bitter
simulacrum of a smile, the girl photographed them
from various angles.

'All right, clothes off,' the prisoners were told,
as the photographer and man laughed and pointed

to their starveling bodies. Silently, the prisoners put on their old clothes again. They had escaped punishment, but they hadn't gained any warmer clothes. Wearing the same tattered garments, the same old clogs, Daniel returned to his shop. It was an effort. His hands shook from nerves and the humiliation of having to smile for the enemy. He was young and still possessed a certain will to live, but he wasn't sure how long he would last under such conditions.

As he was preparing to start work again, the guard on duty surprised him by walking over to his bench and offering him the rest of his beer. Daniel guessed that the guard considered the photographer and official his enemies too, and had found the whole bit with the pictures disgusting. Daniel drank eagerly, thanked the guard and shook his hand two or three times.

The trembling finally stopped, and his thoughts returned to the violin. On the previous days he had finished the ribs and the back; now with a tiny hammer he was beginning to strike, one by one, the minute clamping blocks affixed to the mold. Because he had been careful to use only two drops of luthier glue per block, it didn't take him long to remove the clamps. That ease compensated a bit for the repulsive photographs. He took a deep breath and was filled with satisfaction as he cradled the perfectly shaped object in his hands. He had taken no chances with any of the pieces. The exterior measurements were exact, the same as always. He knew them by heart but checked them again: 355 millimeters long, the breasts (as he called them) 165, waist 115, thighs 205. He couldn't refrain from caressing the instrument he had come to love, the violin that might save his life *if* he managed to finish all the remaining work: the purfling, the scroll, the pegbox, the sound post . . . so many things. Most important, he had to find the proper varnish, all of this before he could assemble the violin.

A tremendous amount of work had to be accomplished before that moment would arrive. He was almost sorry when the siren sounded, for this meant he couldn't begin work on the C ribs. He couldn't risk skipping the meal, however, or doing anything else that would attract attention. It could well be that a fellow worker envied him those two sips of beer! To cheer himself up, he thought about Freund. Then about Bronislaw, who had probably spent all morning cutting turnips and washing pots with hands so delicate they could make a violin sing, hands that one day would move across the fingerboard of the instrument Daniel had crafted at the *lager*. He should be thinking about the musician, not the Commander, who didn't deserve the violin. With this thought in mind, Daniel discovered that his soup tasted better than usual, and he good-naturedly accepted the inmates' jokes about his makeup. He'd completely forgotten about it! He'd have time to remove it that night; it was his turn for a shower. Right now he had to think about lunch.

As often happened at that time of day, Daniel began to recall the meals his mother had cooked for him. The longer he stayed in the camp, the more his mother's image was superimposed on the blurred vision of Eva. His mother and his niece Regina. He remembered walking up the stairs from his workshop, smelling the food, guessing by the aroma what he would be served for lunch: soup with noodles, thick soup, sometimes noodles with chopped walnuts. The table well set, the cheese platter placed to the side on the days that meat was served, following the ritual of separating meat from dairy products. All of that, of course, before the days and months in the ghetto. Now it was turnips and more turnips, turnip soup and more turnip soup.

He felt a friendly hand on his shoulder. It was a fellow inmate, the former professor who was now a baker. The man secretly slipped Daniel a thick slice of bread that he had managed to steal from the bakery. It was dangerous to do so. He could have been killed or whipped, but he risked it sometimes and would offer the stolen morsels to his fellow inmates, following a strict order that was intended to keep others from being envious. Daniel had forgotten that it was his turn! These little conspiracies, in the midst of so much misery, were like flames that warmed the inmates. The professor was fortunate to work in the bakery, but he deserved it; he remembered his friends.

Feeling more cheerful after the extra piece of rye bread, Daniel strode to the heavily guarded row of men who would be taken to the factory. Everyone realized that a truck had just arrived with a new 'load of misfortune.' One of the inmates turned around to glance at it, but a heavy fist sent him staggering; the prisoner started walking faster, eager to avoid being struck again. Let's hope he stays in line, Daniel thought, or they'll kill him just like they did Dénes the other day.

He felt as though he had been in the camp for an eternity, was rooted in it; yet his own arrival seemed like only yesterday. The stupor, the shouts of *Raus!*, the shoves, the humiliating rituals. The long hours of standing naked at attention in the freezing cold, waiting his turn for the miserable, perverse ceremonies: face and body shaved by common prisoners – criminals who wore the terrible green triangles – arms marked by indelible tattoos, hair sheared, bodies disinfected as if they were plants. The fear that the showers might be gas chambers rather than the freezing water that scarified their bodies but was finally inoffensive if the men weren't under it too long. (Sometimes the guards amused themselves by forcing the prisoners to remain in the cold shower until they shook uncontrollably, their teeth chattering.) The thrashings if you didn't immediately understand orders or walked too slowly. The screams and sobs from prisoners whose wives or children were wrenched from them, the defiant eyes of the gypsy who had switched lines and stood by his elderly father while his little boy headed for death.

Daniel trudged along, never pausing in case he too would be struck, but his memory again unearthed the insults issued – at him and at all the newcomers – as he'd descended from the crowded truck, the gentlest being the oft-repeated *bledehunde*, 'You stupid dog!' He thought, as he had that first day, that no response was possible for the terrible suffering, released with such fury against them all on what seemed like an interminable Yom Kippur – the day of abstinence and atonement.

Daniel had thought about his violin for hours, wondered for days about the possibility of his survival. During the Spring Cleaning he had felt more concern for himself than pity for the condemned. But now suddenly, hearing in the distance the shouts directed at the newly arrived prisoners, he marveled that his heart had not completely died, that he could still feel for others, that compassion for other men could spring from him like a tiny blade of grass emerging not from some wasteland but from the rich earth. Despite the derision and his forced smile that morning, despite the months of cold, hunger and threats, his body bruised by beatings, the tremendous effort to stifle the cries when he was whipped, learning not to long for anything, not to think of anything beyond the immediate, despite it all, his heart was alive. He recognized a similar feeling in the eyes of the boy standing in line next to him, a young political prisoner who had just been struck in the face. Daniel silently squeezed his hand, secretly sharing the modest pride of knowing that they had not become subhuman. That was what *they* were.

The guard had moved in front of them now, out of their sight, and Daniel managed to find the energy to comfort the young man.

'Did it hurt much?'

'I can take it.'

Thinking that he had been left too much alone, Daniel put his hand on the boy's shoulder. The youngster – everyone knew everything in the *lager* – had been cut off from his people; he could receive no packages or letters, though he was neither Jew nor gypsy. He had been included in the group for 'supplementary punishment,' what the Nazis referred to by the widely known *secret* name the Decree of Night and Fog. The name itself reflected the perversity of imagination, beautiful words for a terrible practice: leaving the prisoners completely uncertain of everything. Not even the boy's parents knew where he was.

Was it possible that a semblance of morality existed in this world of concentration camps? No, more probably it was simply that they wanted to make the most of the cheap labor that produced such huge earnings. The men in charge of the subsidiary plant of the powerful I. G. Farben had just announced over the loudspeakers that prisoners would be divided into groups for fifteen-minute rest periods. Almost immediately after the announcement, a bonus was distributed among the men, money that could be used to buy food at the canteen. An enormous din, a huge dull clamor like a surging sea, swept through the factory.

'*Schweigt! Still!*' the guards yelled in their attempt to stifle the prisoners' shouts.

The machines finally muffled the sound of human mouths. Daniel's companion was weeping. When it was their turn to go to the canteen, little remained to choose from, and the boy and the violin maker – forgetting all laws other than hunger – attacked a sausage and, like two babes grasping at a breast, quenched their thirst by loudly downing a large glass of milk. When Daniel had swallowed the last drop, he reminded himself that he would need every gram of food he could encounter if he wanted to have the stamina to finish the violin.

VII

Once, God, my dark night had yet to fall
Nor had I suddenly entered upon a strange path.

— JOSEP GARNER, *Nabí*

The violinist began the slow, rhythmic theme of the melody. The bow moved with assurance; soon he would be joined by the simple accompaniment of the violoncello. He had devoted considerable thought to the choice before finally settling on Arcangelo Gorelli's variations on 'La Folia,' in Hubert Léonard's version, a piece he knew by heart. He had made one change: instead of piano or harpsichord, he had chosen the cello for the bass part. They fit together perfectly. He had been wise to select a piece that demonstrated the wide range of the violin's tone quality, displaying string brilliance but no risky acrobatics. Soon the melody danced, bounded. The short fragment of paired notes and trills appeared as the sonata flowed easily, elegantly; then the theme imposed itself again with such beauty that the audience sat in absolute silence.

The cello stopped, and the violin solo concluded the piece. Bronislaw played with great sensitivity and depth. The musician closed his eyes and kept them closed until after the strings had grown mute. Now, he thought in a flash, I'll hear an explosion of applause. He was twenty-six years old, and every concert since his first, at age twelve, had ended in thunderous applause.

He opened his eyes and abruptly returned to the present and his own situation. He was actually surprised to hear a few people – very few – applauding. The Commander himself clapped his hands twice, and the two musicians bowed.

'You played well, it's a good violin.'

Bronislaw breathed a sigh of relief when he heard the words. He was especially relieved because he was conscious that the violin had not been allowed to dry as long as it needed. He noticed that the Commander glanced over at Rascher with an ironic half-smile, a look of satisfaction.

'For the time being, the two of you and the luthier,' he said – no longer referring to him as 'our little carpenter' – 'won't be sent to the quarry.'

The Commander turned to the half dozen guests and said, 'Ladies and gentlemen, they deserve a reward,' as he beckoned to his assistant, who handed him a coin.

Now he'll offer it to me, Bronislaw thought. But that didn't happen. The cellist had left his case open, and the Commander threw the coin in it, as one would for a begging musician. The guests, including a girl in an SS uniform, followed his example. With an expression on his face that showed he was thinking of the food he would buy, the cellist quickly leaned down to retrieve the coins that bore the hated effigy. But no, Bronislaw thought, he would not bend over – unless he was forced to – not after playing with all his soul in defense of Daniel, playing as no doubt Corelli himself would have. His eyes clouded with rage. No, I will not stoop, he thought, and he grasped the precious instrument tightly. For one moment I am a prince.

'What are you doing? Give me that violin!'

Bronislaw held it tightly, then with tremendous regret, his cheeks scarlet with rage, he handed the precious violin and bow to Sauckel, who was exultant as he exhibited it to the others, as if he had made it himself. Bronislaw noticed that one of the guests who had not tossed them any money was observing him with eyes filled with admiration. He had seen the face before, noticed that he was wearing a Wehrmacht uniform, not an SS one; he must have been a well-known musician who'd been mobilized. The man approached and, with no attempt to conceal his action, placed a large bill in the violinist's hand.

'Out of here, now! *Raus!*' Sauckel shouted as he turned around.

The Commander was clearly anxious for the banquet to begin. Delicious food no doubt lay beneath the silver cloches on the white tablecloth. A profusion of flowers, countless bottles of red wine, sparkling champagne glasses . . . as if no concentration camp existed, no war.

Bronislaw – robbed of the violin – and the accompanist with his cello hurried out of the house to change clothes, as they were always ordered to do.

'We'll split the money among the three of us,' Bronislaw told the cellist as he opened the bill to see how much it was.

He found a tiny slip of paper folded inside the bill. On it were written incredible, blinding words, so blinding they seemed engraved in gold: 'I'll get you out of here.' Quickly, he hid the paper from his companion – then swallowed it so no one would know.

Bronislaw finished the piece with the last two strokes: crisp, emphatic and soft, all at the same time. He hadn't performed this piece for a long time, but its melodic contour had taken flight from the first notes, dazzling, never hesitant, perfectly on key. The violinist was the first to realize.

He closed his eyes as he played the final measures; he didn't need to see in order to do justice to the piece. He waited during the brief moment of silence that followed as the air settled. His thoughts wandered from the music: he was wondering if his performance would have satisfied the Commander, if it would have saved his life and Daniel's. The roaring applause banished the bitter mirage. Good Lord, what had happened? Beside him stood a pianist, not the cellist who had accompanied him so many years ago. The two of them took their bows as the stage was strewn with flowers. The applause continued, a standing ovation. The accompanist signaled to Bronislaw to move forward, alone, to take his bow. A beautiful little girl came onto the stage and, with a charming gesture, offered each player a bright red rose, then handed Bronislaw a branch of orchids.

It all seemed like a dream, despite the fact that he had played like a virtuoso, conducted himself with assurance, smiled, signed programs for the melomaniacs who petitioned him, and praised the smorgasbord that followed the concert.

Only then could he return to the peace of his own home, but he wasn't ready to go to bed. He was certain that the familiar nightmare would reappear.

'I'm going to read for a while,' he told his wife Ingrid, who immediately understood. She knew the story of Daniel's violin that her husband had played in the Auschwitz camp. She knew the pain associated with the Corelli sonata.

The heat was turned on and the house warm, but Ingrid had built a fire. He poured himself a glass of cool, refreshing white wine and sat down by the fireplace, something that always gave him pleasure.

He closed his eyes for a moment before he began flipping through the pages of the book he had been reading that week. Maybe it would keep his mind off things, especially today, keep his memories from surfacing. But they were tenacious. It was his fault. He should never have played Corelli's 'La Folia,' a piece he hadn't wanted to perform for years. It carried him back to the *lager*, the image so vivid it was almost a hallucination.

His hair now white, in the calm of his own home, he was finally – after so many years of relative peace – able to confront those memories without trembling. What had become of his companions in misfortune? He almost never talked about that period in his life; he could hardly recall what many of them looked like. He could remember Daniel, however, as if he were standing before him, as if the flames from the fire were illuminating his face. Those eyes that not even hunger could dull – eyes that reflected every movement of his spirit: courage, fear, anger, desperation the day he learned of the bet, him against a case of French wine. He could see Daniel's thin, skillful hands – the backs slightly scraped – the insidious tattoo that both of them bore. Those hands that had waved goodbye to him when he had the immense good fortune to leave the *lager* with an elderly male prisoner and eight sickly women. That was the Dreiflüsselager quota on the shopping list. Yes, Count Bernadotte had bought them – and many more prisoners from other death camps – in exchange for trucks. Bernadotte had run the Swedish Red Cross and had organized the 'white buses' that carried thousands of Jews to Sweden. Bronislaw had always assumed that he had been included on that list because Bernadotte had known the kind-eyed Schindler or the Wehrmacht official who had given him the bill after he had performed for the Commander. My God, what a journey: difficult, never-ending, the devastated countryside, the intense hope. A wild sort of joy, but also regret, a sense of blameless guilt for all those who remained among the Nazis, especially the other two musicians in the trio. Especially Daniel.

Clearly, he wasn't going to be able to concentrate on his book tonight. He put on some soft music but didn't pay much attention to it. Tomorrow evening, after the banquet that was being held in his honor, he would be able to enjoy himself. They were going up to their bungalow in the forest of birch trees, beside a lake where swans and ducks swam. He had never wished to leave Sweden, the country that had welcomed him after Auschwitz. Never. One of the marks the camp experience had left on him was a certain phobia, an insecurity that manifested itself as an irrational fear of travel, of leaving the country. He never felt safe away from his new home, and he soon abandoned the concert tours that provoked nightmares. The exception was an occasional performance in nearby countries: Denmark; Norway; Finland, the land of Sibelius. As soon as he had been given his papers and granted Swedish nationality, Bronislaw had accepted the position of full professor at the conservatory. His rare concerts became quite celebrated. Violinists from around the world visited him to learn his fingering technique and his classical cadence.

No, he decided, I will never again do 'La Folia.' It was the first piece ever played on the violin crafted by his friend, performed before the despised tyrant, performed with all of his being. Bronislaw remembered how he and Daniel couldn't tolerate the idea that the precious instrument would remain in the hands of the Commander; they had even devised impossible schemes to substitute it! It all seemed so recent.

The day after the performance at the Three

Rivers Camp, Bronislaw had found it difficult to calm Daniel. The anguish had resurfaced when he discovered the Commander had announced that the two musicians could continue in their present jobs 'for the time being.' The despicable man had said nothing about the luthier's fate. Had the violin been finished in the agreed-upon time? They thought it had but weren't completely persuaded, and that uncertainty plagued Daniel.

One evening a few days after the performance, Daniel told Bronislaw that he'd been summoned to the Commander's house at noon on the previous day. To his amazement, Sauckel had congratulated him on the beautiful violin. Daniel had stood there, his heart pounding furiously, hoping to learn that he was off the hook and wouldn't be sent to Rascher. Then he'd heard these words:

'I've decided to give you a bonus, even though you did nothing more than comply with your obligation.'

'Thank you, sir.' It had been such an effort to utter those three words. But what came next was unexpected:

'Take him to the kitchen and give him some food. Make it snappy, the factories can't stop.'

The deception was so great it had almost taken Daniel's appetite away, a fact he quickly forgot as he gulped down the plate of stew the cook placed before him. He explained to Bronislaw that, as he'd worked that afternoon, he couldn't rid himself of the idea that the Commander suspected he knew about the bet and was playing with him. But that wasn't all. The day after he had been served the plate of stew, a kapo had appeared at the workshop looking for two carpenters, Daniel and another, younger man. 'Come along with me.'

The two men had put away their tools and followed him as best they could: the kapo was agile, had good shoes and walked fast.

'*Schnell, schnell!*' the kapo had yelled at them, turning around and giving them a shove. 'Hurry up, you lazy bastards, a van has to be unloaded at the Sturmbannführer's.'

So that's it, the luthier had thought, he regrets congratulating me, and now he wants to make me pay for the plate of stew, turn me into a beast of burden to demonstrate that no privileges will be derived from crafting the violin. This wasn't the first time someone had suddenly appeared with orders like this. The two carpenters had been surprised to find Sauckel standing with his dog at the foot of the stairs to his house, beneath the greenhouse filled with plants and blooming flowers, apparently waiting to give instructions.

They'd soon understood: new plants had just arrived. The two men had been ordered to the van, and Daniel had proceeded to unload – one after the other – three huge planters with roses. He wasn't accustomed to the heavy work, and his knees trembled. He was exhausted. After the third trip up the stairs in his clumsy wooden shoes, carrying the heavy plants, he had begun to wobble and felt dizzy. He'd stopped for a moment to catch his breath, and the aide had beaten him on the buttocks with his cane.

'*Ja*, Markus.' The Commander had smiled approvingly. 'Keep them working, they haven't finished.'

As his co-worker carried the last plant upstairs, Daniel had summoned all his strength and crawled to the back of the van, preparing to collect the last load, a large box that had stood behind the planters. Suddenly he'd frozen. His eyes had flickered across the large red letters, his ears imagining the clinking of glasses. It was a case of Burgundy wine. A thick fog had shrouded his eyes, and he had fainted.

* * *

'We won!'

'No, *you* won, you're the only winner.'

They hadn't been able to see each other until that evening. They sat on a rough stone bench, hugging, laughing, weeping unashamedly. No, Bronislaw thought, the Swine didn't win the bet, Daniel did, but at the cost of ruining his health, judging by the look of exhaustion on the luthier's face. The violinist rested his hand on Daniel's fragile shoulder and listened affectionately to the details of the story. They had thrown a glass of cold water on Daniel, and he had regained consciousness. Still lying on the ground, dizzy, and extremely weak, he could hear the Commander and his assistant laughing. The co-worker had finished unloading the van, and Sauckel had allowed him to help Daniel up and accompany him to the infirmary to have the cut on his forehead dressed.

'Take him to be treated, so the frail little man can work this afternoon.'

The taunts didn't bother him. They had won. He had crafted his violin, his Daniel Krakowensis, in the stipulated time.

Now that Rascher was no longer at the camp,

the infirmary functioned much better. Orders had been given to treat all 'curable' prisoners. The Jewish doctor who worked under the German physician did what he could for the prisoners. As the doctor was disinfecting and treating his cut, Daniel whispered to him: 'I won! I won't have to take the cyanide you gave me.'

Daniel had shared his secret with only this person, the taciturn, compassionate doctor who had agreed to give him the cyanide capsule. The day he'd finished the violin, Daniel had purposely cut the back of his hand so that he would be given permission to visit the infirmary.

Daniel described how he had discovered the case of wine and realized that he had won the bet. The doctor shook Daniel's hand and slipped him a box of vitamins, whispering: 'You need them.' Daniel wouldn't have to swallow the poison. He wouldn't be led to a place worse than a tomb: the icy water ruled by the heartless doctor with the treacherous eyes who spied on the agony of the dying.

'The time limit must have been almost up,' Bronislaw told him after a moment. 'So that was why I was given the mornings off kitchen duty and told to help you in the workshop.'

The truth of the matter was that he had hardly helped Daniel. But Daniel had reassured him that just having Bronislaw stand beside him had given him courage. They'd had no opportunity for conversation in the carpenters' shop, other than about the violin. As was only natural, the luthier did most of the work. The musician had served as apprentice: handing Daniel tools, helping him test the different varnishes, grinding the aloe powder with the pestle, putting the fine paintbrushes in the jar with alcohol, wiping with a cloth whenever requested, warming water on the stove to remove excess glue. Small jobs that gave him pleasure.

Bronislaw had stood by and looked on approvingly when Daniel chose the oil-based varnish, observed how carefully he mixed the ingredients (he had forbidden Bronislaw to weigh them on the tiny scales): aloe, sandarac, Venetian turpentine, coloring extract. Daniel had cooked the mixture over a very low flame, then poured it little by little through a gauzelike cloth that he used as a filter. There had been countless tests while Daniel put the finishing touches on the violin. All the odd pieces of spruce and maple lying around the shop bore witness. When the varnished pieces of wood had dried, the two men examined them, scratched them, until finally the luthier's experience – not Bronislaw's – allowed him to choose the most appropriate mixture, though the differences among them were slight. For that matter, Bronislaw didn't even know the exact proportions, but he was able to help Daniel install the four strings and check the tuning.

The euphoria had passed, and Bronislaw scrutinized his friend, who seemed more exhausted than other days. Don't let yourself slip away now, Bronislaw thought. It was time for Daniel to rest; all one had to do was look at the dark circles under his eyes, the extreme paleness of his skin. Bronislaw was determined to find him some extra food in the kitchen, no matter how closely guarded he was. Despite the concern for Daniel's health, they parted happily that night. With the anxiety of the time limit behind them, and the knowledge that Daniel had probably escaped Rascher's grip, Bronislaw hoped the young violin maker would sleep soundly. The night was free from fog, and a tiny star was shining.

VIII

Thick as the leaves in autumn strow the woods.

   – VIRGIL, *Aeneid*, Book VI

The flames were spent, only ashes remained. Bronislaw always felt despondent when the fire was extinguished; the ashes reminded him of the dead. Taking the poker, he scattered them among the tiny embers and poured himself a glass of cool Rhine wine. Ingrid was in bed. Everything had gone perfectly: the tribute dinner, the municipal award. He had noticed some absences, the odd colleague who was sick, another who was probably jealous. Flowers, toasts, medals . . . ashes, everything except music.

What followed had been a tremendous surprise. Neither Ingrid nor any of their friends had
dropped the slightest hint. He still felt deeply moved
and wanted to ponder the events calmly before
going to bed. He would be able to sleep late the
following morning in the calm of the house, with
only the sounds of birdsong and waves lapping on
the lake, like a violin played with a mute.

Ingrid had left the banquet early. 'I'm leaving
now for the lake house,' she'd said, 'to turn on the
heat; my daughter will drive you up.'

Bronislaw had been surrounded by friends and
colleagues, including the director of the opera
house, but by midafternoon it was over and he was
tired, glad he could rest. He closed his eyes as they
drove up to the house and began to feel refreshed.
When he opened them, he could see the glimmering
water of the lake and the well-lit house.

A small group of musicians were awaiting him
and applauded as he entered. He was astonished to
spot the well-known trio: Gerda, Virgili and Climent. He remembered Climent, who had traveled
to Sweden as a very young man to attend one of his
courses on cadence and improvisation. The director
of the conservatory had also come, and a blue-eyed

woman whom he didn't know but who looked vaguely familiar. Everything had been carefully organized. He had no say in the matter; he was led to his seat by the fireplace, Climent and Ingrid beside him.

Then Ingrid put a finger to her lips, and it began. He remembered it all, note by note. He could sing it now if need be. Just the night before he had been thinking how few composers could make a violin sing. They forgot about the melody, the complicity that used to exist between musician and luthier. But tonight all three musicians 'sang.' The novelty, the surprise, had made the first movement fly, but when the violin solo began the second movement, he tried to recall – as he listened, unconsciously retaining every note – where he had heard that sound. After all, this was a trio playing with an unfamiliar woman, and Climent's piece had not yet been performed in public. With a flash Bronislaw realized: the woman was playing Daniel's violin, the Auschwitz violin! He was certain, he didn't need to be told.

When the woman (Bronislaw tended to think of most women as musical notes) concluded the achingly beautiful interpretation of the *Mytilene Trio*, she drew near.

'You see the violin? I was sure you would recognize it. I'm Regina, Daniel's daughter.' She kissed the violin, then placed it in Bronislaw's hands and kissed him on the forehead.

'It's as if I've always known you,' she said.

He ran his eyes over the violin, held it gently. Of course it was his friend's violin that now 'sang' in the woman's hands. He furrowed his brow.

'Daughter? He spoke of a niece.'

The others stepped back so the two of them could speak, and he noticed Ingrid leading them into the study.

'I wanted to forget about it all,' he told Regina, 'but I haven't been able to.' Then he abruptly threw out the question he had anguished over so often:

'Did Daniel survive?'

Without giving it a thought, the two of them broke into Polish – not Yiddish, which the woman had never learned. The luthier had survived the concentration camp, Regina revealed gently, but had died relatively young, when she was only seventeen. After Daniel was released from the hospital, he and Eva had legally adopted her. She became his true daughter; she *was* his daughter. By that time she had already begun to play the violin, she added. Her relative Rudi was a musician, and he started teaching her when she was five.

Bronislaw was elated to meet Daniel's adopted daughter, even if Regina was no longer young. Their encounter was so implausible: she had never before left Poland; he had never wished to return. He had severed all the links to that troubled past, the few that remained from the camp experience.

'I understand,' Regina said. 'Eva never wanted to talk about it either. To stanch the anguish and memories she keeps herself occupied doing a thousand things, drinks a bit too much. She never mentioned it to me, but when I was twelve, Father told me that while she was interned at Auschwitz she had been sterilized in a terribly brutal way. She still suffers from pains in her lower abdomen.'

Daniel, by contrast, had frequently talked to Regina about his experiences, perhaps because he carried with him the knowledge, the glimmer of light among all that misery, of having been able to finish the violin.

All the old shadows seemed to vanish with the woman's voice. When the *lager* was liberated – Daniel had told her – and they were taking him to the hospital, the doctors couldn't understand how he had survived. He spent many months in the hospital, wavering between life and death. The two musicians who had played with Bronislaw died, however, during the first winter after his departure on the 'Swedish bus.' One day, however, after an unexpected visit from his old friend Freund, Daniel had an abrupt improvement, and he was able to fight his way back to life. Her father had given Regina such a detailed account of the visit that she felt she had been present herself.

'Freund suddenly showed up at the hospital and sat down next to Father's bed and with a great flourish exhibited the violin. "It's yours," he said. "I bought it for you."'

It was no mere coincidence, no black-market deal pulled off by Freund, who was on the verge of embarking for the United States. He had actually been able to buy it when they auctioned all the ex-Commander's belongings, shortly after he had been tried and hanged. Rascher, the sadistic doctor-executioner, had committed suicide just before he was going to be hanged. Daniel knew it was his violin. It could be no other. There had been no need to read the letters on it; he carried its exact shape in his mind with the same clarity as that first day, when amid the terror and misery, he had begun to choose the material with which to craft it. Through all the days of hunger, his body often beaten, consumed by rage and grief, in his deepest soul – he told his daughter – he had always hoped that the violin wouldn't be destroyed by Sauckel, that someone, at some point in the future, would save the violin and it would survive, even if he did not.

'You know what?' he had told Regina. 'When Freund brought it to me, it was almost as if I could again hear the question: Occupation? This time my answer would have been: Violin maker.'

No embers remained, only ashes and a lingering warmth from the fireplace. Who knew if he would see Regina again? Bronislaw mused. When she finished the concert tour in Holland, she was going back to her own country. She had returned Daniel to him, and with him a sense of peace. Although Bronislaw had been helpless to do otherwise, it had been tremendously painful to leave Daniel behind in the *lager*, to see him waving goodbye. The memory had tortured him for years.

Climent had presented Bronislaw with the score for the *Mytilene Trio*. Tomorrow he would play the violin part, but if he wanted, he could play it by heart this very moment. That night the old nightmare would not revisit him, the one that always led him back to the Three Rivers Camp.

It isn't true, is it, Daniel, that music can tame the beasts? Yet, in the end, a song lives.